SORCERY & STORIES

A LIBRARY WITCH MYSTERY

ELLE ADAMS

This book was written, produced and edited in the UK, where some spelling, grammar and word usage will vary from US English.

Copyright © 2019 Elle Adams
All rights reserved.

To be notified when Elle Adams's next book is released, sign up to her author newsletter.

1

I lifted the long, thin wand into the air, giving it a wave. Estelle watched me with the same enthusiasm as she had when I'd picked up the other hundred wands I'd tried, but not so much as a spark appeared. The wand remained still, a stick of lifeless wood.

"Ah, well," Estelle said. "Maybe the next one, Rory."

As long as they don't run out of wands first. The assistant who staffed the town's only wand shop had run off to break up a fight between two elderly witches over the last pair of pink wing accessories, leaving us to make our own way through the shop's dwindling collection of wands.

I put the wand back in its case and slid it into place on the towering shelf. A lot of witches and wizards passed on their wands through the family, but Aunt Adelaide had admitted that Dad's wand had gone missing somewhere in the library before his death. Since I'd passed my first round of magical tests early thanks to my aunt pulling some strings at the academy, Estelle had brought me to pick out my wand as this year's Christmas present. I was starting to regret the timing, given the angry yells in the background from the two pensioners at loggerheads over the wand accessories.

Estelle passed me another box with the same patient expression she wore when tutoring undergrad students as part of her PhD in magical studies. Despite our significant difference in magical skill levels, my cousin and I had become close friends in the past month. Estelle and I shared the same curly red hair common to our family, but she'd inherited her curvier figure from her mother, my aunt Adelaide. I had my father's tall, slender frame and pale features, accentuated by the silver-lined black cloak I wore, which was marked with our family's coat of arms. Given my natural affinity for biblio-witch magic, I should have no trouble picking out a wand. Yet every time I tried a new one, an irrational swarm of voices whispering that I'd never belong here in the magical world struck up a chorus, breaking my concentration.

"Maybe they can sense my nerves." I held up the new wand and waved it. A pathetic hissing noise came out the end.

"Wands can't sense feelings," Estelle said. "Our family has a unique type of magic, so it's only natural that you might be drawn to an unusual wand."

The wands all looked exactly the same to me—sticks of wood shaved down to the same shape and size, bare of accessories. Imagining my cousin Cass's face if I had to admit none of the wands wanted me made me shudder. Carrying a magical pen and notebook and an inventory full of words which contained magic might be impressive enough on its own, but a magic wand was the symbol that would indicate my acceptance into the paranormal world as a whole. Small wonder my nerves were through the roof.

"Come on, I picked out a familiar with no trouble," I whispered to the stick in my hand. "A wand shouldn't be that hard to choose."

"That's it." Estelle's eyes lit up. "Why not ask Jet to help you choose a wand?"

"I suppose it couldn't hurt." I'd opted out of bringing my crow familiar to the wand shop with me, figuring he'd get overexcited, but we'd been here almost an hour. Putting the wand back into its box, I raised my voice. "Hey, Jet, can you give me a hand?"

The shop quietened. Then a rustle of wings sounded and my little crow familiar flew into view, landing on the shelf in front of me.

"What may I assist you with, partner?"

"I'm trying to choose a wand," I said. "I wondered if you could have a look and see if any appeal to you?"

The crow had sensed a bond between the two of us, so maybe he'd be able to sense which wand was best-suited to me.

"Certainly!" Jet took flight for the shelves, causing the boxes to rattle.

"Aren't you done yet?" The teenage shop assistant appeared, looking frazzled. One of the wand-wielding pensioners had hit him with a quick-grow spell and a huge moustache and bushy red beard now adorned his face.

Fighting a giggle, Estelle used her own wand to reverse the damage. "There you go. Sorry about them."

"Thanks," he said. "Why is there a crow in here?"

"He's my familiar," I hastened to explain. "I thought he'd be able to sense which wand resonates with me."

The assistant dragged a weary hand through his now normal-length hair. "I hope my supervisor doesn't see him. He's paranoid enough about the Magpie."

"Magpie?" I queried.

Shooting a worried look over his shoulder, the kid dropped his voice. "The police are trying to keep it quiet, but they suspect a notorious thief is hiding in town. He's wanted across the country for stealing from prominent magical communities, and he's known for leaving a magical signature in the shape of a magpie behind wherever he strikes."

"I didn't know," I said, with a nervous glance at the trembling stacks of boxes.

"Your aunts will," he said. "They'll want to keep the library safe from his sticky fingers."

Jet emerged from the stack of boxes and offered me a wand, which I took.

"Don't worry, the library's well-protected." I gave the wand a wave, and a feeble spark shot from the end. "Is that it? Did it choose me?"

"No," said the shop assistant, a frown on his face. While I sympathised with him, considering he'd spent the morning breaking up fights between parents determined to get their children the best wand accessories for Christmas, his obvious impatience made me feel even more frustrated.

"There must be *one* wand that works for me," I said. "It's not possible for none of them at all to choose me, right?"

The shop assistant didn't answer, but a shadow fell

over the shelves from behind me. I turned around as an elderly man came into view, leaning on a walking stick. Like the assistant, he wore the uniform of the wand shop—a red robe emblazoned with an emblem of three wands crossing. Was he the shop's owner?

"You're the new girl," he observed. "Aurora Hawthorn."

"Um, yes." *Please tell me he didn't just see me get rejected by over a dozen wands.* "I just passed my theory exam and I'm here to pick a wand."

"So you are." His gaze went to Jet, then to the towering shelves of boxes. "I am Mr Hale, the owner of this shop. Outsiders do sometimes have trouble picking out a wand, but I can only think of one occasion where the wizard failed to connect to any wand at all."

My stomach sank. "So it *can* happen?"

"Very rarely," said the grey-haired man. "It was a long time ago… and now I recall, I'm not so sure the man was actually a wizard. Occasionally, people break the rules and smuggle in their non-magical friends or partners. It's rare that they try to claim a wand, but on this particular occasion, I believe the individual ultimately decided to leave town."

Calm down, Rory. That's not you. You've already proven you're a real witch. "You mean someone brought in a—a normal, who couldn't connect with a wand?

"They did," he said. "You're not the same, because you're *from* a family of witches. You share their talent, so connecting with a wand should—hey, stop that!" He waved his walking stick in the direction of another fight.

The assistant spun on his heel and ran to calm down the brawling shoppers, while the old man sighed. "The whole town has gone mad."

Estelle and I ducked behind the shelf to avoid being hit by a flying box of wand accessories. With a muttered curse, the elderly supervisor retreated into the back room while his young assistant attempted to break up the fight.

"Did your mum mention anything about this thief?" I whispered to Estelle.

"She may have," she said. "He'd be a fool to steal anything from the library, though. We've upped our defences. If anyone takes our possessions outside of the town, it'll have some pretty nasty rebound effects."

"Good." I straightened upright, returning the wand to its place on the shelf. When I'd first used biblio-witch magic, I'd been filled with a rush of confidence. I didn't walk through the magical world expecting everything to work as directed, but I was sure that holding my first wand was supposed to feel less—deflating.

Estelle handed me another wand. "Try this one."

I waved the wand. The lights flickered, but the wand felt odd and bumpy in my hand, not comfortable like I did when I used biblio-witch magic.

"Relax," said Estelle. "Imagine you're Aunt Candace when she finishes a manuscript."

"What, annoyed and at a loose end, looking for an argument?"

"Okay, bad example." She smiled. "What about when she has an ingenious idea for a new book?"

"Inspired by one of us?" I raised the wand.

She gave a mischievous grin. "I'm sure she'll end up writing an epic romance between a reaper and a biblio—joking, joking," she added, as I gave the wand a wave. I'd been meaning to set off a stream of sparks, but the wand made a noise like a deflating balloon.

"Maybe I need to get you riled up instead," she said. "Or—oh hey, Mum."

"Did you say Aunt Candace?" asked Aunt Adelaide, appearing from behind a display. "Have you seen her? She went to 'get some air' two hours ago."

"She did?" Strange. Aunt Candace spent almost every waking moment in the library. I rarely saw her set foot outside, especially when she was in the middle of a new project like she was at the moment. Maybe she'd gone Christmas shopping, but she hated crowds even more than I did.

"That's odd," said Estelle. "Did she say where she was going?"

"Does she ever?" Aunt Adelaide shook her head. "It's bad enough the police are on the lookout for that thief… she'd better not be pestering them to answer questions for research again."

Ah. That does sound like her.

"Wait," I said. "If you and Aunt Candace are out… then who's in charge of the library?"

Aunt Adelaide's expression shuttered. Then she about-turned and left the shop, sweeping past the bewildered-looking assistant. I didn't blame her—if Cass was left to watch the library unsupervised, the day generally ended with illegally-acquired magical creatures running amok all over the lobby.

"Ah." Estelle turned to follow her. "Rory—you can stay and pick out a wand if you like."

Jet flew past with a shriek as a torrent of sparks shot from the wand accessories section. Two shopping-bag-laden witches squared off, and the assistant stood between them, his knees trembling.

Deciding that I'd rather deal with whatever chaos Cass had created in the library this time than get caught in the witches' standoff, I put the last wand back into place and made my way out of the shop.

Scores of shoppers packed the high street, caught in the pre-holidays rush. Glittering Christmas trees filled the windows, decorated with snow that looked real and never melted.

Estelle and I caught up to Aunt Adelaide at the town square. "I'll find your aunt," she said. "You two… make sure the patrons haven't turned one another into spiders."

"Gotcha," said Estelle. "Don't worry, we've got it under control."

The library towered over the square, a majestic red-brick building with stained-glass windows and a pair of tall oak doors—a sight that never ceased to take my breath away. I could hardly believe it was mine, even the trick staircases, disappearing floors, and the invisible upper floor that nobody had been able to access for years. Not to mention the vampire sleeping in the basement and the owl who was secretly the embodiment of the library's entire store of knowledge. My former job as a bookshop assistant under my dad's grumpy former business partner, Abe, seemed a whole world away from the library's chaotic yet welcoming atmosphere.

On the ground floor, towering shelves filled the space beyond the front desk, while wooden balconies formed five stories, climbing until they disappeared from sight. In the centre stood a vast Christmas tree decorated with flashing baubles, while glowing lights draped the balconies and fake snow glittered on the shelves. Having seen my aunt conjure up an actual snowstorm using the library's magic on one memorable occasion, I was glad she'd opted for the fake option.

In the Reading Corner—a cosy space filled with bean bags, hammocks and comfy chairs nestled at the back of the ground floor—a number of patrons cowered behind an overturned desk. On the other side, my cousin Cass stood beside a tall, spindly creature, speaking in a murmur. Estelle's younger sister had the same long red hair as the rest of us, currently twisted into a topknot. Her pale, freckled features matched mine and my dad's, while her willowy figure was more like Aunt Candace's. She wore the same long coat as Estelle, with the sleeves rolled up and covered in what looked like mud and tree bark.

As we approached, the creature hissed, turning to face us. He had elongated features, long limbs, and sharp-looking teeth.

"What," said Estelle, "is that?"

"He's a boggart," said Cass. "He's scared of loud noises. Don't move."

The patrons didn't move a muscle. The boggart towered over them, his spindly hands reaching out. Cass tapped his wrist firmly and he shrank away.

"He doesn't look scared," I whispered. "He looks like he's about to eat someone."

"It's a defence mechanism."

The boggart howled, the sound echoing throughout the Reading Corner. As one of the patrons made a run for it, his spindly hands reached out again, grabbing the teenage wizard by the leg and dragging him along the carpet.

Oh, no. Wishing I had managed to claim a wand, I

pulled out my Biblio-Witch Inventory and tapped the word *fly*.

The boggart left the ground, hovering in the air. The wizard he'd tried to grab gave a grateful nod, scuttling out of sight. My book vibrated in my hand, resonating with the magic humming inside me. Thanking the hours I'd spent practising, I turned to Estelle. "Is there a cage somewhere here?"

"I'll fetch one." She whipped out her own wand, waving it in a complex motion, and a cage appeared beneath the boggart, catching the creature's spindly form within it. "Sorted."

Cass whipped to face her sister. "You're frightening him."

"I think he'll survive it," Estelle said. "What were you thinking? Mum left you alone for five minutes, if that."

"I didn't let him out the cage," she said indignantly.

"Even if you didn't, you brought him into the library to begin with." With another flick of her wand, Estelle locked the cage door. I made a mental note to learn that one as soon as I had a wand of my own. In a library where half the doors were marked with an X—designating them as forbidden and dangerous—one could never be too careful. I'd had to ask for Sylvester's assistance the last time I'd needed to lock the door on a rampaging magical creature—in that case, Cass's pet manticore.

Estelle caught me looking at her wand. "Don't worry," she whispered. "It took Aunt Candace a while to find a wand she liked, too."

"But you all chose your wands when you were what, five years old?"

Yet another way in which I stood apart from the rest

of the magical world. Dad had grown up here, but he'd had to leave this life behind when he'd married Mum. I'd grown up not having the slightest idea that magic was real, so it was no wonder that my acceptance into this world had hit a few snags.

"Well, yes," she admitted. "But you're new. And besides, you passed your exam. Full marks, Mum said."

My face heated, while Cass gave a snort. "They haven't changed the syllabus in years. And where's your wand? I thought you were going to buy one today. At least, that's what you've spent the last week going on about, so I assume you were."

I frowned at her. "I've mentioned it twice at most. I only found out I passed the exam yesterday. And I didn't even get to buy one before someone decided to let her pet out of its cage."

My aunts had taken me under their wing for tutoring in biblio-witch magic, while potion-making, casting spells and magical theory lessons were squeezed into any spare moment I possessed. I was also supposed to be starting familiar training, since I'd decided to bolster the bond between myself and Jet and accidentally gave him the ability to speak instead. But without a wand, I was still cut off from half the magical world, and despite my resolve not to let Cass's taunting get to me, I couldn't help feeling disappointed.

"I told you," Cass said through gritted teeth, "I didn't do it. Aunt Candace is the one you should be worried about, if she's loose in town without supervision."

The boggart howled and rattled the cage bars. It wasn't the first time Cass had brought a magical animal from outside and tried to take care of it in the library, but the

Magical Creatures Division was all the way up on the third floor. I'd improved my levitation skills, but last time I'd tried levitating a cage down three floors, the kelpie had escaped, chased the patrons, and then rampaged through the town square. Considering the town was in a frenzy over last-minute Christmas shopping on top of general end-of-term stress, they might need the entertainment, but it wasn't fair to put any more pressure on Aunt Adelaide. Especially with Aunt Candace up to her usual mayhem.

"Where'd you even find a boggart?" Estelle asked Cass. "I thought they avoided people."

My cousin shrugged. "Magical creatures like me."

The boggart tried to lunge at her through the cage, which fell over. I raised an eyebrow. "You sure about that?"

Cass flicked her wand and returned the cage to its rightful position. "I told you, he gets nervous around strangers. I'll take his cage back upstairs."

"I thought you promised you weren't going to bring any more of those creatures into the library."

"He was already in the library." Cass gave her wand another flick. Since the boggart was a lot smaller than the kelpie the two of us had once levitated downstairs, the cage glided smoothly up the staircase.

"What do you mean by that?" I followed, holding my Biblio-Witch Inventory in case she needed backup. "*Where* in the library?"

"Boggarts like cold, dark places," she said. "I found him in the Relics section. He's probably been there for weeks."

The boggart rattled the cage bars. I tapped the word

rise in my Biblio-Witch Inventory and its path steadied, carrying it up to the second floor.

"Then shouldn't you call pest control or something?" The boggart gave another lunge, almost tipping the cage over in mid-air. "Or whatever the magical equivalent is? There's got to be someone you can call when you get a nest of pixies in the attic or gnomes in the garden—"

Cass shrieked, tripping backwards at the sound of a monumental clang. The cage had collided with something solid—or some*one,* human-height and decidedly hairy. He toppled over sideways onto the stairs, bellowing obscenities.

"Cass, the cage!" I tapped the word *rise* to steady the cage before it tumbled downstairs.

Recovering, Cass levitated the cage past the unexpected obstacle, towards the closed door at the back of the third floor. I, meanwhile, leaned over the newcomer, hoping we'd only stunned him. He wore an odd silver jumpsuit, which looked like it might belong to an astronaut. Or a convict. *Oh, no. Please tell me Cass isn't collecting prisoners as well as rare animals.*

The man sat up abruptly. "How dare you attack an officer!"

"Excuse me?" I said. "Who are you?"

"I am Captain Wayfarer, and you are charged with attacking my squadron."

That sounded like a load of gibberish to me. "I think you got hit on the head. Were you looking at the books?"

"Books?" He looked around, wearing a baffled expression. "I haven't seen paper books in many years. Is this a museum?"

"No, it's a library," I said. "Where did you come from?"

"Up there." He jabbed a finger upwards, but there wasn't anything there except for the white-painted ceiling.

"What, through the ceiling?" Why did I run into all the nutcases? I glanced around in search of Cass, but she'd disappeared along with the boggart's cage "Do you want to come downstairs and speak to my cousin? She's in charge of, uh, hospitality."

"Very well," he said. "Take me to your Cousin of Hospitality."

Oh... kay. Baffled, I made for the stairs, hoping the others would have better luck making sense of our strange new visitor.

Cass came out of the boggart's room. "Why is there a werewolf in here?"

Oh, is that what he is?

"He claims he's lost," I said.

Cass snorted. "Don't tell me—he wandered in here after a night at the pub and can't remember how to get home."

The man—or rather, werewolf—turned on her with narrowed eyes. "My crew will be on their way to assist me soon. Then you'll be sorry for insulting me."

"He's not making any sense," Cass said.

I know that. First a boggart, now a confused werewolf. Why had I given up my chance to buy a wand? I should have known I wouldn't manage to avoid any havoc until the new year.

Aunt Adelaide waited in the lobby, her arms folded over her chest as an apologetic Estelle attempted to calm down the patrons. Nobody spotted the werewolf until he let out an angry bark from behind my shoulder. "Who are these people? This isn't the station."

"Excuse me, who are you?" said Estelle. "You're a werewolf, right?"

That's when a dozen huge wolves leapt over the balcony, landing in the middle of the ground floor.

2

"I told you my allies would soon arrive," said the wolf triumphantly. "Now you will pay for speaking ill of the captain."

"Don't look at me," said Cass, staring at the wolves. "I've no idea what's going on in here."

That makes two of us.

I'd never seen a werewolf in the flesh—or fur—and I hadn't realised how much bigger than normal wolves they were when they transformed. There were strict rules governing shifting in public, and unlike vampires, I hadn't studied werewolves in enough depth to know how to subdue one, let alone half a dozen of them. Even Estelle and Cass stood frozen in shock.

The central werewolf forward and transformed into a man… a *naked* man. A soft gasp came from Cass, while Estelle averted her eyes. I did my level best to keep my eyes on his face as a stunned hush fell over the library. Not only was he stark naked, he resembled the sort of guy you only saw on romance novel covers and in action movies. The others shifted to human form too, one by one. All naked, all—let's face it—gorgeous. *Okay, this is far too weird.*

"Who are you?" Aunt Adelaide demanded of the first werewolf, who thankfully still wore clothes. "Which pack do you belong to?"

"Pack? I am the captain of the Wayfarer squadron." He turned to my aunt. "You're the leader of this base, I assume? What do you call this place?"

"The library." Aunt Adelaide looked between him and his nude companions, wearing an expression of disbelief. "If you're here to threaten us, you'll find the library isn't without its own protection. You have been warned."

"We are not here to threaten you," said the man. "We're merely here to find our missing crew members."

"There are more of them?" Cass wore a smirk on her face. "Let's invite them here, and ask them all to shift into human form, too."

"Cass!" snapped Aunt Adelaide. "Shifting in a public building is against the law. What kind of pack leader wouldn't know that?"

"How dare you imply that I am not fit to lead my pack?" The werewolf's voice was a rumbling growl. "We have travelled here from our prison at great risk."

"Prison? You broke out of jail?" Aunt Adelaide looked as though she was about to explode. "Right. All of you, stand there. No, there. And Estelle, please fetch these werewolves some clothes. We're losing business here."

"Pretty sure we can get half the town to come in here if we tell them we have a bunch of naked werewolf visitors," Cass said in a loud whisper.

I choked on a laugh. "You didn't kidnap a werewolf pack, Cass, did you?"

"No, of course I didn't bloody well kidnap a werewolf pack," she said. "They just appeared from nowhere."

"A likely story," said Aunt Adelaide. "Tell me your name, pack leader."

"My name," said the werewolf, "is Captain Wayfarer."

Estelle snorted. "Uh, that's a name from one of Aunt Candace's books. Nice try."

The werewolf growled. "This is not our home. Which quadrant is this?"

"I told you," said Aunt Adelaide, "you're in the library. If you don't give me a reasonable explanation for your being here, I'll have to call the leader of the local shifter council. They don't take kindly to finding trespassers on their territory."

"This territory belongs to another?" said the werewolf. "This is not a museum, is it?"

Estelle blinked in bewilderment. "No. Rory, *where* did he come from?"

"Cass and I found him on the stairs near the third floor and accidentally hit him with the boggart's cage," I said. "Maybe he hit his head too hard."

Cass snickered. "He even *looks* like Captain Wayfarer. He's the spitting image of the main character from *The Adventures of Werewolves in Cyberland.*"

Estelle's eyes widened. "You know… he is. How many wolves does he have at his command, twelve?"

"And don't they all look like supermodels?" A calculating expression stole onto Cass's face.

Aunt Adelaide pulled out her Biblio-Witch Inventory and tapped a word on the page. At once, the bookshelves moved, caging the werewolves between them. They set up such a cacophony of howling that the remaining patrons backed towards the exit.

"Quiet," Aunt Adelaide snapped. "Tell me who you are and who sent you here."

"We know who they are," Cass said, fighting a laugh. "It's Captain Wayfarer and his crew of misfits, exploring cyberspace on grand adventures."

"I didn't know you'd even read that book," Estelle said. "I'm glad one of us finds this amusing, but I'm still totally lost. Are they like... paid actors?"

"No, they walked out of one of Aunt Candace's books," said Cass.

"What, you mean *literally* walked out of one of her books?" I asked. "Is that even possible?"

When would I learn not to ask that question in a library where the impossible was routine? Okay, cyberspace-travelling werewolves were a bit much even for us. The books in here might be more mobile than I was used to, but I'd never seen any characters walk *out* of a story before.

"If you'd paid attention, you'd know," Cass said. "Mum's wasting her time trying to find out what pack they belong to when they're not even real."

"They look real to me." Estelle turned to the gawking patrons. "Did one of you summon those wolves?"

There was a chorus of 'no's. The library's remaining visitors were mostly witches and wizards, all looking baffled and scared, with one exception. A tall man with the same muscular build as the visiting werewolves pressed his mouth in an angry line, glaring at the newcomers.

"Is this a joke?" he said to Estelle. "Has your family been hiding a rogue pack of werewolves in the library?"

"Of course not," Estelle said. "They're clearly under a spell. Or *from* a spell, assuming Cass isn't having us on."

"If they came out of the book, shouldn't we be able to get rid of them if we find a copy of *The Adventures of Werewolves in Cyberland*?" I asked.

Cass snorted. "Good luck. The library contains dozens of copies of each of Aunt Candace's titles, and even she doesn't know where all of them are."

Great. "Well, we ran into the first guy on the stairs, so it's worth having a look around there."

When Cass didn't reply, I cast another look in Aunt Adelaide's direction. From her frazzled appearance, the werewolves were not answering her questions to her satisfaction. *Where* did *they come from?* Maybe this Captain Wayfarer character had suffered a hard blow to the head, but that didn't explain where his fellow crew-mates had materialised from. I'd never read that particular book of Aunt Candace's, so the details were lost on me.

Since nobody objected, I hurried up to the third floor. The Magical Creatures Division existed on that floor, so it was no surprise that the trouble had come from there—though werewolves weren't classified as 'creatures' in the magical world, since they were humans who could transform into beasts. From what my magical education had covered so far, I gathered that they only transformed on nights of the full moon, so the fact that they were running around in wolf form in here meant they were breaking some of the magical world's strictest rules. No wonder my aunt was so ticked off.

On the other hand, if they *had* walked out of one of the

books, then presumably they'd disappear once one of us found the source of the spell. Given all the other bizarre wonders the library contained, a magical section that brought fictional characters to life wasn't *that* unlikely. I'd seen weirder in my first few days alone. It sounded like the sort of thing that would be shelved behind one of the locked doors—most of which were helpfully marked with X symbols—or else hidden away in one of the 'advanced' sections. So, definitely not something I was equipped to handle alone.

"Hey, Jet," I called, realising I'd run out of the wand shop without checking my familiar was following me.

The crow swooped into view. "Danger!" he said. "Wolves, wolves, so many wolves!"

"I know," I said. "I'm trying to track where they came from and I could use some backup."

The third floor looked much the same as usual. Cass had left the boggart's cage in front of the half-open door at the back, which led to the rooms where she kept her other acquisitions. Judging by the growling coming from in there, the ruckus had woken her pet manticore. At least the door was locked.

The boggart hissed and rattled the bars at me, but I ignored him, pacing through the shelves to check the rest of the third floor. Hisses and growls pursued me, along with the occasional snapping noise. Half the shelves came equipped with thick gloves so we could handle the books without losing a finger. Some shelves were encased in thick glass to protect the books—or to protect any unwary passers-by—and others were covered in so much fur, it was impossible to tell if the werewolves had passed this way or not. I circled the floor, Jet flying at my side.

"I can't make heads or tails of this," I admitted to my familiar. "It's like they just popped out of thin air."

"Popped out of the air, out of the air!" he proclaimed, taking flight with a shriek as one of the books swiped a claw at him.

Despite the shelves' eccentric collection of tomes, I found no copies of Aunt Candace's extensive backlist. Nor any secret passageways or hidden stairs that suggested the wolves had been hiding in the walls or ceiling. The only clue was an abundance of long grey hairs on the floor, which didn't prove anything.

"Sylvester?" I called out, my voice echoing. "Can you give me a hand over here?"

I didn't expect the owl to answer. My family's other familiar was more elusive than ever, and it wasn't uncommon for him to vanish for several days at a time. Ordinarily I'd be relieved he wasn't around to mock my failure to acquire a wand, but he had an uncanny knack for vanishing whenever we needed his help.

Jet landed on my shoulder. "I can't find it, partner."

"No worries. Can you go and look for Sylvester?" Even if the owl himself didn't show up, this bizarre situation seemed an appropriate time for a consultation with the Room of Questions. Not that I was supposed to be making a habit of using it.

After giving the floor another scan, I walked downstairs to find the other patrons had left the library, while the bookshelves caging the wolves into place had moved aside. Ropes bound each wolf's hands and feet. All were in human form, and at least half of them appeared to be asleep. Most of them were still naked, too.

"You're not actually turning them into a permanent

fixture, are you?" I asked. "If we're going with the Christmas theme, I suppose they could hold Santa hats in strategic places."

Cass cracked up laughing then covered it with a cough. "Some of us would appreciate it."

Estelle giggled. "Check out the goods while checking out the books."

"Honestly, you three," said Aunt Adelaide. "Fictional or not, they can still hear every word you say. Did you find anything useful?"

"It looks like the werewolves appeared on the third floor," I said. "There were hairs all over the Magical Creatures Division, but no sign of any of Aunt Candace's books."

Cass made a sceptical noise. "Half the books have hair in that section."

She wasn't wrong. "Where's Sylvester, anyway? You'd think he'd be getting a good laugh out of this."

"No idea," said Estelle. "Maybe he's frightened of werewolves."

Aunt Adelaide made an impatient noise. "This won't do at all. None of the people present in the library cast the spell, so I had no choice but to allow them to leave. But they'll talk, and before the day's end, the entire town will know we're harbouring a lawbreaking werewolf pack. If anyone has a confession to make, now is the time."

"I didn't do it," Cass said.

"I believe you," said Aunt Adelaide. "This has Candace's name written all over it."

"Is that why she took off?" said Estelle. "Bringing her own books to life? What's she playing at?"

"Maybe if I call the police, she'll have an incentive to

come back," Aunt Adelaide marched away to our living quarters.

That seemed unlikely. If anything, Aunt Candace had enjoyed her last stint in a prison cell. The police, not so much.

Cass rolled her eyes after her mother. "She doesn't believe me."

"Cass, really," said Estelle. "Of course Mum believes you, though that'll change if you let those wolves free."

"I wasn't going to," she protested, putting her wand in her pocket. "I just thought it would be good for business."

"Not if everyone's busy with last-minute Christmas shopping," said Estelle. "Aunt Candace would find it hilarious to bring her werewolf characters to life and set them loose in the library, but I don't understand why she didn't stick around to watch the fallout."

Hmm. "Because she knew Aunt Adelaide would skin her alive?"

"And guess who'll take the punishment?" grumbled Cass. "Aunt Candace could get away with murder and our mother would forgive her and punish me instead."

"You wouldn't take the punishment if you didn't break the rules," Estelle pointed out. "I thought you got rid of the manticore."

"I did. That was a boggart."

"You didn't," I said. "I heard it growling. Unless that was another werewolf."

Cass looked alarmed. "I can't let them hurt my pets."

Backing away from the werewolves, she took off for the stairs at a run.

"I'm pretty sure it was her manticore I heard," I said. "Though half the books growl up there, too."

"They do at that," said Estelle.

One of the werewolves made a low noise, more wolf than human. The ropes seemed sturdy enough, but those guys looked like they packed a punch even in human form. "Are they actual people under a spell, not illusions? They sure *look* real."

"You know… good question." She frowned. "You can't create something alive using a spell, but there are detailed illusions and transformation spells. My mum tried a dozen reversal spells and all we managed to do was keep transforming them from human to wolf and back again."

"So you think the spell will wear off by itself?" I asked.

"I *hope* so."

There was a crash, and the sound of Cass swearing from upstairs. Aunt Adelaide strode into view a moment later. "I'm not helping her. She needs to learn her lesson at some point, and she at least has more sense than Candace does."

"She's right," Estelle said, in a low voice. "Our mother comes down so hard on Cass because trying to get Aunt Candace to obey any order is like putting a harness on a manticore. Cass will grumble to the ends of the earth, but she'll do as she's told eventually."

"Where *is* Aunt Candace, though?" I said. "It's not like her to leave the library at all, let alone with everyone caught up in shopping madness. Unless she's hiding in a secret passageway laughing at us."

"Not if my mum saw her leave." Estelle frowned. "Summoning a pack of wolves and then hiding away is more the type of thing Sylvester would find amusing, not her. Granted, she was in a foul mood this morning…"

"Maybe that's why." I walked over to the werewolves,

most of whom were draped in cloaks Aunt Adelaide had conjured up from the spare room. They sure didn't *look* like they'd come here on purpose.

The leading werewolf made a growling noise. "As part of the official code, you are forbidden from holding hostages," he said. "I demand that you release us."

"You're not hostages," I said. "Technically, you're trespassing."

"There is no property in cyberspace."

Nobody would put this much effort into an elaborate prank, right? I made a mental note to scan the contents of the rest of Aunt Candace's books so I'd be prepared the next time one of her characters ambushed me. "Where *did* you come from? Do you remember... a book?"

He looked at me like I had three heads. "This library of yours contains nothing *but* books. Are all humans so dense?"

"Don't speak to my niece that way," said Aunt Adelaide.

"I was trying to find out if he remembers having a spell put on him," I explained. "If they're not illusions, they might be real people who've been enchanted to believe they're fictional characters."

"Perhaps," said Aunt Adelaide, "but I wouldn't tell Edwin that, otherwise he won't take them off our hands. I'd prefer for certain other paranormals not to find out, too, especially Evangeline and the vampires."

I suppressed a shudder at the sound of her name. Considering one of her vampires had died in a case I'd been investigating, a bunch of humans had attempted to rob her, and then I'd blocked her from reading my mind the last time we'd seen one another, I'd be quite happy not to set eyes on the leader of the vampires for the foreseeable future. Vampires had a literal eternity to hold grudges, after all.

Thankfully, the werewolves and vampires were natural enemies and there was zero chance a vampire might be involved with whoever had conjured up a werewolf pack straight from Aunt Candace's novel. Compared to the vampire-related trouble I'd dealt with, the werewolf situation was laughable.

The library doors opened, and two trolls entered, flanking Edwin, head of law enforcement in the town of Ivory Beach. He did not look pleased. "What is going on?"

Aunt Adelaide hastened to explain, while Estelle and I kept a close watch on the werewolves to ensure nobody tried to make a run for it. The elf police chief was just over four and a half feet tall, dwarfed by the two trolls he employed as security guards. The trolls, lumpy grey brutish figures wearing blue cloaks, were friendly enough, but I still took a step back as one of them bared his jagged teeth at the werewolves.

"You're saying they're *not* werewolves?" Edwin scanned them. "Why aren't they wearing clothes, then?"

"It's a little complicated," Estelle said.

"And how am I supposed to arrest people who might be the creations of a spell?"

"Same as anyone else," I said. "They won't know the difference."

Edwin approached the wolves. "You all broke the law, so I must punish you accordingly."

"We broke none of the known laws of cyberspace," he said. "You have no reason to incarcerate us here."

"What is he talking about?" said Edwin.

"He's under a spell," Aunt Adelaide said.

"This is absurd," said Edwin. "We have quite enough to be getting on with without a horde of werewolves appearing in a public library. Is he drunk?"

"No, he's a fictional character," answered Aunt Adelaide. "Created by someone who thought it amusing to turn a book into reality. I'm not entirely sure if he's a construct or a real person who's been led to believe he's acting out the events from the book—that is, *The Adventures of Werewolves in Cyberland.* My guess is that Candace left a copy lying around somewhere and a spell affected the pages, but it's mere guesswork."

His eyes widened. "Candace wrote that book?"

Oops. I think her secret pen name might be out.

Aunt Adelaide didn't seem particularly bothered about outing one of her sister's secret identities. "Yes, and it appears someone found it amusing to bring her characters to life. I need to track down my sister, but I felt it set a bad precedent to allow the werewolves to rampage around the library, real or not."

There was a pause. "Do you know if your sister will sign my copy?" asked Edwin.

3

"This town has officially gone bananas," Aunt Adelaide announced that night at dinner. "Two wizards got into a fight over the last bottle of elven wine at the market. One of them was turned into a toad, and the other has been whistling non-stop ever since."

"And might one of those people have conjured up the werewolves?" I asked.

Cass continued to shovel food into her mouth, ignoring everyone, while Aunt Candace still hadn't returned from her 'errand'. Aunt Adelaide, having concluded that being mobbed by people begging her to sign their books would be punishment enough for now, had left her to it.

"Unlikely," said Estelle. "The wolves came *from* the library, right, Mum?"

"Perhaps," Aunt Adelaide said. "That, or they're the product of a powerful spell—or curse. Granted, curses usually have a target."

"The curse did have a target," Cass said. "Us."

"Maybe someone felt threatened by that escaped boggart," I said. "And used the only defence they had—the books."

"None of the people present in the library had the skills to cast a spell like that," my aunt said. "Even *I* have difficulty seeing how it's possible. I checked the Dimensional Studies Section, but if any of the doors were unlocked, they aren't now."

A dangerous book escaped at least once a week, so if anything, it was surprising that a living person hadn't stepped out of a book before now. The library was known to be semi-sentient, courtesy of my grandmother, its original creator. The werewolves, though, appeared to be individuals, and not part of the library itself.

"They didn't actually come from another dimension, though," I said. "They just *think* they did. Because in the book, they go into cyberspace... and they think the library is a museum."

"Because paper books don't exist in their reality," said Estelle. "You know, every word they've said has been consistent with the book."

"That doesn't prove anything," said Cass. "Aunt Candace walked into a hostile spell in here once and went through a phase of thinking she was a cat."

"That's not the same," Aunt Adelaide said irritably. "Edwin keeps sending me lists of questions as though *I* have the faintest idea where these wolves materialised from. They keep talking utter nonsense at him."

"It's not nonsense, Mum," said Cass, with a smirk. "It's the law of cyberspace. Besides, I'd be happy to listen to them talk, especially the guy with the chest hair."

"That's enough, Cass."

The door to the kitchen opened and Aunt Candace walked in.

"There you all are," she said. "What did I miss?"

There was a long, awkward pause, during which Sylvester swooped in and landed on the table. So that's where he'd been all day. Weird. I'd never known him to accompany Aunt Candace anywhere before. Unless she'd recruited him on some dastardly scheme. Given the expression on her face, there was a slight possibility. It was probably my fault for loaning her Jet on days where I was too busy or tired to listen to his enthusiastic tales of the town's gossip, so she'd become used to having the help of a familiar.

Aunt Adelaide glowered at her. "Your dinner is in the oven, Candace. Might you please enlighten us on where you've been today?"

Aunt Candace flicked her wand, opening the oven and levitating her plate over to the table. "Why is everyone staring at me?"

"Have you seriously not heard?" Cass rose to her feet. "We got attacked by Captain Wayfarer and his crew."

"Is that supposed to be a joke?" Aunt Candace dug into her food. "Because nobody aside from your sister even likes that story."

"And Edwin," Cass added.

Aunt Candace turned to look at her niece. "Edwin? You told him I wrote *The Adventures of Werewolves in Cyberland?*"

Cass put down her fork. "Yes, I did, when your werewolf pack came to life and were running amok all over the library. I suppose it's fortunate for all of us that it was just the werewolves and not the giant robots. Or the tentacled monsters from your Lovecraft parody."

Aunt Candace looked around at all of us. "You're all playing along? Even you, Adelaide?"

"It's true," Estelle said. "A bunch of werewolves showed up thinking they were in cyberspace. Thirteen of them, like the crew."

"They appeared from nowhere," I added. "We're not sure if they're not real or if they're just regular people under a spell, but poor Edwin has drawn the short straw and has them incarcerated until we figure it out."

Aunt Candace put down her fork and rose to her feet. "Why, I shall have to see them."

"Not so fast." Aunt Adelaide moved to block her path. "Where exactly have you been all day?"

Her sister blinked. "There's no need to talk in such an accusing tone. You leave here on errands all the time."

"You never do, Candace. That's why."

"I heard an old friend was in town, that's all," said Aunt Candace. "She's a reporter now, and she's come to nose around and get up to mischief. We met at university, before I decided journalism wasn't for me."

"You went to university?" I asked.

"Don't sound so surprised," she said. "If I planned to bring my characters to life, I'd have picked a better book than that one."

"Are you sure?" asked Cass. "They were all totally naked, by the way. We were thinking of letting them come back as assistants when they get out of jail, to improve business."

Aunt Adelaide blew out a breath. "You're all going to drive me into an early grave."

"Hey!" said Cass. "I'm not the one whose book characters are running around the police station."

"Did she set the boggart loose, by any chance?" asked Aunt Candace.

"How did you guess?" said Estelle.

"I saw her carrying its cage up to the third floor earlier this morning."

"Did you know the werewolves also appeared on the third floor?" Aunt Adelaide enquired.

"The boggart had nothing to do with the wolves!" Cass insisted. "The werewolves aren't even real. Nobody ever criticises Estelle or Rory's hobbies."

"None of us would object to your hobbies if they didn't try to eat the patrons," Estelle pointed out. "I'm going upstairs. Coming, Rory?"

Recognising a chance to get out, I followed her out of the kitchen. "I'm actually heading out to meet Xavier in a bit."

Her eyes rounded. "Where are you going?"

"For a drink," I said. "At the Black Dog pub. Though the way things are going, a swarm of werewolves will barge into the bar to join the karaoke night."

"Is Xavier singing?"

"I never asked," I said. "There's probably some Reaper's rule against it."

Hadn't stopped him from asking me out, though. While we'd spent plenty of time together over the last few weeks, this was the first time Xavier had explicitly asked me to go out with him to an event that ticked every 'date' box in the book. It might not seem like a big deal, but the prospect of potentially facing the shadowy Grim Reaper again made me feel more nervous than trying out wands had.

A knock came from the door, and I drew myself upright, taking a deep breath. "Okay, I'm heading out."

"Have a great time!" Estelle called after me.

I waved back at her and opened the door to greet Xavier. The Reaper's apprentice stood on the doorstep, dressed in black as usual. His golden hair and aquamarine eyes made him look more like an angel than you'd expect of a guy who carried a huge scythe strapped to his back, but that was probably an advantage in a job where he had to escort hysterical ghosts into the afterlife.

"Hey, Rory," he said, in his deep voice.

"Hey." I closed the door behind me as Aunt Adelaide and Aunt Candace's argument rose in volume. Glad I wouldn't have to stick around to see the outcome, I hopped off the doorstep.

Xavier and I walked down to the seafront. Today's events aside, I'd begun to settle into life here in the library —and in Ivory Beach as a whole. The seafront had grown as familiar as the high street where I'd used to work. The town's nightlife, if you could call it that, occupied one side of the road facing the beach and mostly consisted of pubs rather than clubs. Witches didn't come to this small town to party, though in summer, they held barbecues on the beach and funfairs on the pier. Magic didn't extend to control over the weather, so rain and sleet were the order of the day, and we were more likely to have a damp Christmas than a white one. A cold breeze whipped off the coast, making me shiver, but Xavier's Reaper abilities ensured he didn't feel the cold.

A large tree had appeared on the pier overnight,

draped in fake snow. Christmas music—mostly remixes of familiar songs, as well as some unfamiliar ones—blared out of every bar and pub.

"I didn't know the paranormal world was so big on human holidays," I remarked.

"It depends," said Xavier. "A lot of us celebrate the solstice, but traditions from the human world creep through in places like this. The town used to be a human resort before it was gradually abandoned. Then paranormals moved in and fixed up the place until we outnumbered the humans, and this was the result."

Hmm. "You said 'we'. You've lived here that long?"

"No, but my family has."

I didn't know much about Xavier's family, only that his father had been a Reaper before him and that had somehow led to him being chosen to take on the same job. As long as he carried the scythe, he couldn't age, so he might theoretically be old enough to have lived in the town since its creation. But he didn't act at all like the vampires, who were also ageless, suggesting he was younger than his immortality implied. I'd never quite got up the courage to ask.

Whispers followed us into the pub and as we sat at a table near the door. Xavier gave me an apologetic look, but I was used to stares, whether I was alone or not. Perks of being the town's newest witch—and the lost cousin, according to the dedication in the book Aunt Candace had written detailing my dad's epic romance with my mother. Really, I should be glad *that* wasn't the book which had come to life in the middle of the library.

Xavier took a seat. "I don't know if you've been to a

restaurant or bar here before, but you just tap the menu to order whatever you like."

"Nice." I picked up the menu, skimming through a list of unfamiliar cocktails. "Any recommendations?"

"The marshberry whirl is a popular choice."

"Might as well live a little." I tapped my fingertip to the entry on the menu. "So I just wait for it to appear?"

He tapped his own menu with a fingertip. "Shouldn't take long. There are more people here than I expected, what with it being the end of term."

"Mm." I wasn't big on crowds. Since I'd led a fairly solitary life and then moved to the library, which was vast and echoing so it never seemed crowded, the pub felt uncomfortably cramped. Still, the company was more than worth it.

Our drinks appeared on the table. Xavier picked up his beer glass and took a sip.

"Does the alcohol have any effect on you?" I asked. Thanks to his Reaper powers, he didn't need to eat or sleep, in theory.

"Not really," he replied. "But I like to keep up appearances."

"You should challenge those students to a drinking contest."

He grinned. "There'd be no competition. Same with any sporting event. Not that I'm allowed to take part, for that reason. No swimming event would be fair if one of the participants can breathe underwater."

It seemed there were a lot of things the Reaper wasn't allowed to do. "And karaoke nights? Are you allowed to take part in those?"

"Nah, I'm tone deaf."

"There has to be one thing you're not brilliant at." Ack. That sounded like I was trying too hard to flatter him. Even if it was true.

Feeling my face heat, I looked away from the table and spotted the shifter who'd been in the library when the werewolves had made their unsuccessful bid for freedom. He scowled at me.

Xavier followed my gaze. "Why is that guy looking at you?"

"Let's just say my aunt Candace has reached a new low." I launched into an explanation of the day's events. He howled with laughter at my tale of the werewolves' dramatic appearance in the middle of the library.

"They're in jail?" he asked. "I bet poor Edwin isn't taking it well."

"He seemed more interested in getting my aunt's autograph." I grinned, sipping my drink. "I think that's the only reason he didn't lose his temper. Aunt Candace will be annoyed that another of her pen names is public knowledge, but if she's responsible for bringing those werewolves to life, it serves her right."

Xavier drained his beer glass. "For the record, I already worked out it was her who wrote that book. She has a distinctive style."

"I didn't know you'd read that many of her books," I said.

"My boss doesn't keep any books at home, so I've been visiting the library for years." He put down his glass. "Anyway, that werewolf book is one of the wackiest things she's written. It's not surprising that she'd think it would be funny to bring the captain and his crew to life."

"I'm not a hundred per cent sure she's the one who did

it, but she's not exactly behaving in an innocent manner," I said. "Either way, poor Edwin deserves compensation for arresting a pack of cyberspace-travelling werewolves who don't actually exist."

He smiled. "True. His troll guards have been busy breaking up fights for last-minute Christmas purchases all day."

"Yeah, a couple of elderly witches got into a brawl at the wand shop earlier." I sincerely hoped we wouldn't have to greet the festivities with a flood of characters from my aunt's books. The werewolves were bad enough on their own.

"Oh yeah, how did the wand shopping go?" he asked.

"Not great," I admitted. "None of the wands I tried out resonated with me. And then Aunt Candace's werewolves interrupted, so we had to dash back to the library."

"Ah," he said. "I'm sure you'll find one that works for you when things are a bit less chaotic."

"I hope so," I said. "I wasn't supposed to be starting proper wand lessons until January anyway, but I tried dozens of them and even Jet couldn't find one that would work for me."

The shop owner's story about the person who'd never found a wand chose that moment to nudge its way into the back of my mind. *Stop that.* I wasn't a normal. I'd made great strides with my biblio-witch magic over the last few weeks and had even managed to make my familiar able to talk. I'd get the right wand eventually.

"I wouldn't worry too much about it," Xavier said. "You were distracted today. Warring pensioners doesn't sound like a pleasant backdrop to choosing a wand."

"It might have helped if I'd been able to use a shield spell." My smile faded. "Maybe I'm expecting too much, but when I picked up the wands, I never got the feeling I do when I use biblio-witch magic. I can't describe it, but it just feels—right."

"I get it," he said. "I'm not a witch, but I understand."

It's the feeling I get when I look at you. The thought came before I could stop it, and I was glad I'd dressed for the weather in a thick scarf so he couldn't see the flush creeping up my neck.

"Anyway, I'll go back there after the holidays." I glanced up as the shifter gave our table one last glare, then left the pub. "Maybe take Jet along again."

"I'm sure it'll be fine," he said. "This isn't the typical wand-buying season, so there isn't as much of a selection. They might buy more in the new year."

If there was one thing I loved about Xavier, it was his unrelenting faith in me.

"I hope you're right," I said. "Anyway, enough about me. How was your day?"

"I had to pull out my scythe to break up a fight outside the boss's gates," he said. "Two wizards got into a brawl over a box of fairy lights."

"People even started a fight right next to the Reaper's house? I didn't know the vampires were that big on Christmas decorations." I drank the last of my cocktail. "That must be handy, being able to casually pull out the scythe whenever you like."

"It does make walking through crowds considerably easier," he said. "There are perks to being utterly terrifying."

"Terrifying? You?" Come to think of it, the tables

around us were notably emptier than they'd been when we'd entered the pub.

"They're scared of my boss," he corrected. "I don't take it personally. Besides, I meet all sorts of interesting people at work."

"Do people typically chat to you when they're on the way to the afterlife?" I asked.

"You'd be surprised. One guy the other week was adamant about finishing the book he'd been reading before he died. I may have stalled my boss to give him the chance to reach the last page."

"I knew I liked you for a reason."

"Is that the only reason?"

His words carried an undercurrent I hadn't expected, and a flush rose to my cheeks. Before I could reply, a loud chorus of growls came from outside.

"I think," I said, "the werewolves may have escaped."

"I thought so." He dropped a stack of coins on the table, which instantly vanished. The magical way of paying for things was handy for those of us who preferred to keep interactions with strangers to a minimum.

At the sound of shouting and thunderous footsteps, we ran out of the pub. I expected to see werewolves sprinting around the beach, but instead, two of Edwin's guard trolls ran towards the clock tower, their huge feet thumping on the pavement.

"It's not the jail," Xavier said. "Something else must have happened."

We hurried down the road leading into the town square. A clamour echoed from the high street, and the trolls lumbered that way without slowing down.

Xavier and I exchanged concerned glances. *What's going on this time?*

We reached the entrance to the high street and halted. The front of the wand shop was a mess of shattered glass, surrounded by a growing crowd. The teenage assistant from earlier stood in the ruins, staring through the wrecked window.

"He just—disappeared," he was saying to the police guards in a shaky voice. "He ran too fast. I didn't see where he went."

"One of the wolves broke into your shop?" I asked.

"No," he said quietly. "It was *him.*"

Xavier's grip on my arm tightened when I stepped forwards, seeing a glowing symbol on the window, shaped like a bird.

"The… Magpie." I recalled the name of the thief rumoured to be in town. "What did he take?"

"One of our best wands."

Xavier moved to my side. "We should leave before Edwin shows up."

Before he blames my family for it. Not that the werewolves were in any way connected with the thief. *Right?*

4

A tremendous screeching noise woke me the next morning. Groaning, I opened my eyes. Sylvester sat on the bed post, his large tawny wings spread in the manner of a peacock, and said, "What light from younger window breaks?"

"Did you seriously wake me up at the crack of dawn to quote Shakespeare at me?" I yawned. "Also, it's 'But soft, what light from yonder window breaks?'."

"There's no need to be pedantic."

"I have a Masters in Classical Literature," I said. "I know that's not quite as impressive as being the living embodiment of the library—"

"As a matter of fact," he said, "I came to inform you that the werewolves have gone. They disappeared at the stroke of midnight, much to the displeasure of the law enforcement officials who spent the night filling out unnecessary paperwork."

"At least they aren't causing trouble anymore." I

slumped back against the pillows. "You might have let me sleep in first."

He ruffled his feathers. "I wanted to ask you for a favour."

Uh-oh. Sylvester had never asked me to do anything without a price. "What exactly?"

"Your aunt," he said, "has sneaked out of the library again. I'd like you to accompany me to follow her."

"Why not fly yourself?"

"My magical ability is limited outside of the library's boundaries," he said, with a great deal of dignity. "You may have gathered that your aunt Candace can be a little unpredictable. I believe she's up to something she doesn't want Adelaide to know about."

"And that concerns you… why?"

"The library concerns me," he said. "Something has been out of place here since yesterday."

"If you mean the werewolves, are you saying Aunt Candace activated the spell herself?" I wouldn't have thought she'd have spent all evening denying it if she had, but he was right in saying she was unpredictable.

"She's up to something," he said. "I thought you might accompany me to find out where her so-called errands are taking her. I tracked her down at the beach yesterday evening, but she refused to say where she'd been all day."

Hmm. It was fairly obvious that like Cass, he was only asking me because I was the person most likely to say yes. On the other hand, if even Aunt Adelaide hadn't managed to get her sister to admit to causing the spell, perhaps I might be able to talk some sense into her.

Curiosity won out. "All right, but you owe me one for this. Say… a free visit to the question room. No tricks."

"Well, all *right.*" He flew out of my bedroom. Hoping I wasn't making a mistake, I pulled on my clothes, tugged a brush through my hair, and grabbed my bag. Ten minutes later, I hurried downstairs to meet Sylvester in the lobby. It was too early for anyone else to be awake, so I made a mental note to grab a muffin on the way back and walked out into the bitterly cold wind.

Even the most hardcore late Christmas shoppers wouldn't be outside in this weather. The air stung my face and numbed my ears, prompting me to quicken my pace. Sylvester flew at a sideways angle to keep from being swept out to sea.

"There she is," he said. "This had better be worth losing half my feathers in this ghastly breeze."

In front of us, Aunt Candace paced down the road leading to the seafront, walking with purpose. Her hair blew across her face, even wilder than usual, and she halted below a row of balconied windows at one of the seafront hotels.

"What is she doing?" I came to a halt a few feet behind her, ducking behind a lamp post so she didn't see me snooping. Sylvester grabbed the lamp post with both clawed feet, the wind ruffling his feathers the wrong way.

"I have no idea," he said. "I saw her pacing around the area yesterday, too. If I didn't know better, I'd say she's spying on someone."

"That's Frederick's place." The owner of the local hotel seemed nice enough, but I was pretty sure spying on the guests wasn't allowed. If this was an attempt to get material for a new story, she was pushing her luck. Aunt Candace often took liberties with the rules, but spying on strangers was downright bizarre behaviour even for her.

"Wait, is this about that 'friend' of hers who arrived in town? She mentioned someone from university, and I think she said she was a reporter—"

A scream sounded from one of the rooms upstairs, cutting off my words.

"How *dare* you?" a female voice screeched. "Did you think I wouldn't catch you kissing her in the stairway?"

"I—I—" The sound of a man's protests drifted through the window. "It wasn't what you thought."

"I *saw* you," screamed a woman. "Don't you dare deny it, Steven."

"I think we might have interrupted a couples' spat," I remarked to Sylvester. "Oops."

Aunt Candace spun around, looking directly at our hiding spot.

"Liar! Cheat!" screamed the woman.

"Oh, dear," said Aunt Candace, summoning her notebook and pen. "Pity. People enjoy their drama."

"It doesn't sound like anyone's having much fun in there," I said, not bothering to hide. She was the one who had some explaining to do, besides.

"You brought the owl to spy on me, did you?" said Aunt Candace.

"*You* were spying on the guests at the hotel," I pointed out. "You could get into a lot of trouble for that, you know."

The screaming grew louder, and my aunt stepped away from the window. "No, I think I already wrote an argument similar to this one. Unless I turned one of them into an alien. Or a werewolf. I don't *think* I've already done that one…"

"What is wrong with you?" I asked. "You even worried

Sylvester, which is an achievement. I didn't think he cared."

"That's not a nice thing to say," the owl said indignantly, not relinquishing his clawed grip on the lamp post. "Maybe I'll stop caring about all of you."

"We know you love us really, Sylvester," I said, and he huffed. "Anyway, Aunt Candace, I don't know what you're playing at, but you must know what your sister will say if I tell her you're spying on people. I'm certain Edwin doesn't want you anywhere near his jail ever again."

"I'm not intending to get myself arrested," she said. "Ursula Hancock is—"

At that moment, the hotel's upper window flew open and a wizard tumbled out headfirst, waving his wand at the last second to break his fall. He bounced once, twice, then landed on his feet. "She threw me out!" he protested.

Aunt Candace snapped her attention onto him, her pen quivering with excitement. "Oh, dear. How unfortunate."

I gave an exasperated sigh. "You're not going to tell me you're responsible for that, too?"

"Don't be absurd." She moved out of the way of the window, at a safe distance from any more flying wizards. "I didn't tell him to kiss his ex-wife in the stairwell, did I?"

"I think it's about time we went back to the library," I said, having had about enough. "The werewolves disappeared in the night, did you know?"

"Oh, good."

The wind whipped Aunt Candace's hair across her face as she turned away from the hotel and strode towards the town square. Sylvester let go of the lamp post and flew over my head, while I hurried after her. She was surprisingly fast for someone who spent most of her time hunched over a writing desk.

"Aunt Candace," I panted, "where is your copy of *The Adventures of Werewolves in Cyberland?*"

"Which copy?" she asked. "The new one or the original draft?"

"She means the one that summoned those werewolves," said Sylvester.

"If I knew that, dear, I would have handed it to my sister when she hurled accusations at me all evening." And with that, she whipped through the door into the library.

I stopped walking. "I'm going to buy a muffin for breakfast. Sylvester, can you make sure she doesn't sneak out again?"

"This isn't my job," he grumbled, but he obligingly flew towards the library.

I, meanwhile, darted across the road to Zee's place. Her cake shop had quickly become one of my favourite places in town, a haven of heavenly smells and mouth-watering tastes. Iced buns sat in rows, new pastries appeared every day, and Zee's special berry-flavoured muffins seemed to taste better every time I tried one.

Zee, the owner, had warm brown skin, generally covered in flour, and long curly hair made curlier by the heat.

"Hey," I said. "Don't mind me, I'm just going to stand over here in the warmth for a while to recover from the cold."

She laughed. "Try one of these buns. They warm your whole body in an instant. Oh, and you can reheat them later if they cool down."

"You're a lifesaver." I handed over enough cash for five

and held the bag to my chest as I left her shop. The first bite of the bun sent warmth shooting straight to my toes. Even my annoyance at Aunt Candace melted away in the flavour of delicious berries.

I walked into the library, humming to myself. Nobody was on the front desk, so I put the bag of buns down and checked the logbook. It didn't *look* like anyone had recently checked out a copy of *The Adventures of Werewolves in Cyberland,* but since the spell appeared to have been used in the library itself, they wouldn't have needed to. In any case, the spell's absurd side effects seemed to be over for now. *Thank god for that.*

I looked up at the clock above the door. Nine-fifteen… and the library wasn't open. Weird. Aunt Adelaide was normally punctual to a fault.

"Hey, Aunt Adelaide," I called through the door to our living quarters. "Isn't the library supposed to be open by now?"

No reply.

"Aunt Candace?"

My other aunt didn't respond either. She must have gone upstairs. Frowning, I caught sight of Sylvester sitting on a shelf above the desk. "Where are they?"

"Don't ask me. I'm in charge of late fees, not opening hours." He ruffled his feathers. "Well, as scintillating as spending time with you has been, I'm off to find somewhere warm to take a nap."

The owl snatched one of the buns out of the bag on the desk and flew away over the bookshelves. *Great.* Maybe Aunt Adelaide had slept in. Or perhaps she'd gone looking for her sister. I finished my muffin and went to search the ground floor. Not so much as a hair remained of the werewolves, nor any sign of the spell that had summoned them.

Oddly, the lights remained dim. I'd thought they switched on automatically, but it must be the library's magic at work.

I cleared my throat, facing the impressively towering five storeys of balconies and the shelves beneath. "Lights on."

Nothing happened.

"Lights," I said, louder, my voice echoing in the empty space. "Turn on."

I've lived in the library long enough for it to trust me, right? The lanterns came on by themselves in the evenings and the library seemed to do everything on autopilot, but I couldn't help feeling wrong-footed that my words had no effect.

I manually switched on the light over the front desk instead. Heaps of books lay piled on tables waiting to be returned to the shelves, and a strange empty feeling hung around the whole area. Aunt Adelaide wasn't there all the time, but the entire library felt different without her here.

My heart beat faster as I ran towards the living quarters. Nobody was in the kitchen making breakfast, or in the living room. I checked every corner, then made for the staircase to the upper level.

Footsteps sounded above me. "Hey, Estelle, is that you?"

A startling *neigh* answered, and the sound of hooves beating echoed downstairs. I yelped and flung myself out of the way, in time for a knight on horseback to sail past me into the lobby.

"Hey!" I shouted after him. "Who are you?"

More to the point, what was he doing in my family's living quarters? *And just how did that horse get up the stairs?*

The horse wheeled on the spot, its rider leaning down to look at me. "Fair maiden, I apologise for startling you."

My mouth dropped open. "Uh… who *are* you? Where did you come from?"

"I am Sir Woolworth, of course."

Oh, no. First werewolves, now horse-riding knights. Was this another side-effect of Aunt Candace's spell? "Uh, wait a moment, I'll just get my aunt—"

The front door opened, startling me. While the library might not be operating as usual, everyone knew it opened at nine—and of course, there wasn't a sign on the door saying my aunt had disappeared.

"I'll be right back," I told the knight, and ran to the front desk.

A young Asian woman and a tall blond guy looked around the dark lobby in confusion.

"Er, excuse me?" the woman said to me. "Are you open?"

Argh. Why did you have to run off and leave me to deal with this, Aunt Candace?

"We're having… technical difficulties." Wherever Aunt Adelaide was, she wouldn't want the library to fall to pieces in her absence, but it would be nice if someone showed up with an explanation. "My aunt's fixing the problem, but everything should be in working order."

The horse cantered into view with a loud *neigh,* making both newcomers jump violently.

"I thought he was a statue!" gasped the woman. "He's real?"

"Yes, he is," said the horseman in self-important tones.

"And might I add, you are the fairest maiden I have ever laid eyes on?"

Horror washed over me. *Okay, this is worse than the werewolves.*

"Maiden?" she said, giving an uncertain laugh. "Is this a show?"

"He's playing a part," I said quickly. "Uh, we're thinking of starting a drama club here in the library, since the poetry club is so popular. We're trying out historical figures. My aunt will be here in a minute." Or she'd better be. None of my library training had taught me to deal with living book characters wandering around hassling our visitors and bringing animals into the lobby.

"Oh," she said. "Who exactly is he supposed to be."

My mind was blank. "He's… Sir Landon. From *The Adventures of the Man and His Horse*. It's very popular in the normal world."

Really, Rory? That's the best you can do? Nobody said I was any good at thinking under pressure.

Hearing a coughing laugh from behind the counter, I turned around. "Sylvester, you can come and help now. Which book did you want?"

The owl swooped down to land on the desk, and the woman gave another startled jump.

"Hello," he said. "What can I do for you?"

"She's terrified of birds," said the blond man. "I'm sorry, but we're going to have to leave."

The knight leapt down from the horse. "I will save you, fair maiden, from the hideous creature that attacks you."

"How *dare* you," howled Sylvester, spreading his wings wide. "Get out."

The man and the woman backed to the door and fled outside as the owl flew in a screeching circle around the knight.

"Hey!" I said. "Can you not scare off our visitors?"

"Fair maiden, I only wanted to assist." The knight bounded back onto his horse, and I suppressed the urge to knock him over the head with a textbook. I had to get rid of him—but how?

"I realise you're under a spell," I said through gritted teeth, "but you're not supposed to be here. Sylvester, can you find Estelle and Aunt Adelaide? Aunt Candace is around, but I doubt she'll be much help."

He clucked his beak. "Trying to get me to do your dirty work again?"

"You owe me for yesterday." Could even the book of questions get to the bottom of this catastrophe? It seemed a waste of a question to jump in there and ask where my family members were hiding, but I was worried about all of them, even Cass.

"Fine," he said, and swooped away, leaving me alone with the knight. I put my head down on the desk and groaned.

"Fair maiden, I detect that you are a little stressed."

"Please stop calling me that." I lifted my head. "Jet, where are you?"

Please say he hasn't vanished as well.

To my relief, the crow flew down to the desk a moment later. "Hello, partner!"

"Have you seen the others?" I asked him.

"I saw your cousin Cass leave the library an hour ago," he squeaked.

Figures. "All right. Can you watch the front desk? If

anyone comes in, say we're closed for... cleaning. Also, this guy likes to hear the local gossip, and he'd love it if you updated him with everything that's happened in the whole town in the last week."

"With pleasure!" he squeaked, flying to land on the horseman's shoulder.

I left the two of them to it and walked outside, mentally cursing Aunt Candace. I didn't have the faintest clue which book that knight had walked out of, but I was willing to bet it had her name on it. Or one of her pen names, at least. The last thing I wanted was to leave a demented knight and a gossipy crow in charge, but if I didn't get someone to help me deal with this mess, I'd never be able to open the library.

As I'd predicted, I found Cass on the pier, standing beside the towering Christmas tree. What I didn't expect was to see *two* kelpies wheeling around the shallows while she looked on, wrapped in her long cloak. The second kelpie was smaller than Swift and lacked the same white-blue mane, meaning she was female. I'd learned a fair bit when researching them while Swift had lived at the library, but they weren't native to this part of the country. Still, lost horses were the least of my problems today.

"Hey," I said. "Cass, I need your help. The library's supposed to be open and everyone except for Aunt Candace is missing."

She turned to me, her eyes shining. "Swift found a mate. I thought he'd never find another kelpie here."

"Is that so?" I glanced at the kelpies, who frolicked around in the shallows. "Cass, I'm sorry to burst your bubble, but I think Aunt Candace's spell has reached the next stage. There's a lunatic on horseback in the library babbling about fair maidens."

Cass's mouth dropped open. "You what?"

"You know the werewolves disappeared overnight, right?" I said. "Well… it doesn't look like the spell is over. Is there a story of hers which involves a knight on horseback, by any chance?"

"Maybe one of her historical romances?" she said uncertainly. "I'm not familiar with that pen name, but Estelle is. Where is she?"

"I haven't a clue," I said. "The library didn't open itself like it normally does, and Sylvester and the knight got into a fight and scared off our only patrons."

"Oh." She closed her mouth. "Okay, I'll go and… help. Now you mention it, I think I saw my mum heading that way." She pointed over her shoulder.

"You didn't think to ask her to stop?"

"I assumed she was running an errand," she said. "Unlike Aunt Candace, she usually comes back. Where's *she* hiding, anyway?"

"She's looking for the book that started all this." Not that it made a difference if a different story was playing out before our eyes.

The loud sound of several horses neighing rang over the rooftops. Oh, no. What now?

With Cass on my heels, I broke into a run, heading towards the town square. To my horror, no fewer than seven horses circled the square, each bearing an armoured knight. Two of the knights were jousting with spears, while another was eating a muffin no doubt pilfered from Zee's bakery. Yet another knight emerged from the flower shop carrying a bouquet of roses.

"This can't be happening," I muttered to Cass. "This is just... too much."

The nearest horseman rode to my side, dropping roses everywhere. "May I offer you a rose, fair maiden?"

"Nope," I said firmly. "Not interested."

"I'll take one," Cass said, wearing a smirk. "Lighten up, Rory. Unless you're saving yourself for Xavier. I wonder if he's appeared in a book yet?"

The knight handed her a rose, then offered me a bouquet of other flowers. "Please, fair maiden, select the flower you would prefer."

"Go away," I muttered, hearing a crash behind me. I ducked into the nearest shop and found Alice struggling to put her pets back in their cages.

"Those knights didn't come after you, did they?" I asked.

"They tried," she said. "I told them I like women, so he promised to rescue an extra princess from a tower just for me. And then my cats chased him off."

"Oops," I said. "As you've probably gathered, this is my aunt Candace's fault. The knights are from her romance pen name's books."

"I didn't realise she wrote romances."

Given the state of things, I doubted Aunt Candace would care that everyone in town would know all her secret pen names. "I'm going to sneak out again. Wish me luck."

To my annoyance, the flower-carrying knight was still waiting outside, and he pursued me all the way to the library's doors. "Does another man have your heart, fair maiden?"

The image of the Reaper came to mind. *Oh well, it*

might get him to leave me alone. "Yes. I can't give you what you want." *Mostly because you either don't exist or are under a spell. Not that it matters, because I have a crush on the one guy I can't have.*

"If you change your mind..." He threw the roses after me, and they scattered on the porch.

I entered the library, finding a bemused-looking Estelle standing at the front.

"There you are," she said. "I've been looking everywhere for you, Rory. The library rearranged things again and locked me in a cupboard."

"I'm glad you're here," I said. "Help yourself to a bun... they might have gone cold by now. It's been one hell of a morning."

Estelle listened with wide eyes as I detailed the events of the day—roses, knights and all.

"Oh, no," she said. "I'll have to think—which book are the knights from?"

"I haven't read any of her romance pen name's books," I said. "I've only read her sci-fi and fantasy adventures so far. I'm guessing the knights were from a historical romance book? There's a lot of 'fair maidens' going around, and one of them threw roses at me. Did Cass come back in here?"

"Yes." Cass ducked out from behind a shelf. "That owl wouldn't leave me alone."

"I did tell him to find all of you."

"That explains why he helped me out of the locked room." Estelle finished her bun. "Aunt Candace, though... are you sure she's not responsible?"

"The library didn't even open. We're losing business." I shook my head. "She told me she was going to look for the book that caused all this, but if it's affecting more than one of her pen names, perhaps just one book won't be enough. Also, how are we supposed to open the library with a jousting contest blocking the doors?"

"We'll have to close it for the day," she said. "At least until my mum comes back—"

The door opened. Aunt Adelaide strode into the library, her hair in disarray and a distant, wistful expression on her face I'd never seen her wearing before. "Oh, Estelle, Rory, there you are."

"Mum, what are you doing?" asked Estelle. "The library's supposed to be open, and you weren't here. Where did you go?"

"It was for a good cause," she said. "A great cause, in fact. Your father and I have decided to get back together."

5

"You're joking," Cass said. "Mum, please tell me you're joking?"

From the way her eyes were shining and the dishevelled cast to her appearance, Aunt Adelaide was not joking in the slightest. And not mentally present either.

"Aren't you going to open the library?" I tried. "I don't know if you noticed, but there's a bunch of horsemen stampeding around the town square throwing roses at people—"

"True love waits for nothing," she said.

"Oh, god," said Cass. "She's turning into Aunt Candace."

"I'm sorry, Aunt Adelaide," I said. "But I think you're under Aunt Candace's spell. I'm guessing she wrote a romance novel in which a divorced couple gets back together?"

"Excuse me?" She blinked at me, some of the mistiness vanishing from her expression.

Maybe I'm getting through to her. "The spell that brought the werewolves to life yesterday," I went on. "Remember? Today, it's playing out Aunt Candace's romance novels—possibly all of them at the same time. There are horsemen rampaging around trying to sweep women off their feet, couples arguing at the hotel..."

"I've been thinking about it a lot," she said. "And when I woke up this morning to find Elliott outside my window—I just had to go and talk to him. It turns out he's been thinking exactly the same, can you believe it? We talked it over, and we decided, well, why wait?"

"Mum," said Estelle, her voice quiet. "What are you talking about?"

"We're getting remarried, of course," she said.

"You're not serious, are you?" said Cass. "You can't have forgotten how you used to argue every single day. And what about the library? Remember when it locked him in the Nature Section for two days? He hated this place."

Aunt Adelaide gazed dreamily into the distance. "The library is the perfect location for us to declare our love."

"Just—hold on," Estelle spluttered. "Mum, trust me when I say I'm not trying to wreck the mood. You're under a spell."

"Or a curse," added Cass. "Did someone think this would be funny? Are they playing a joke on our family?"

"Not just us," I said. "Even the kelpie wasn't spared."

"He can come to the wedding, too," said Aunt Adelaide.

For the second time that day, Cass's mouth fell open. "You've lost your marbles."

"It's Christmas," Estelle said, looking equally stunned.

"Everyone's busy. Why not wait and decide after the holidays are over?"

"There's no better time than this to celebrate family." She wrapped her arms around all three of us at once. Cass's face looked like I imagined it would do if Sylvester chewed through her favourite book.

Releasing us, Aunt Adelaide paced around the desk, humming happily. "This is the perfect season for love and good cheer."

"Really," said Cass. "I thought it was the perfect season for everyone to trample one another to death over presents."

"Honestly, Cass, you're lacking in any holiday spirit." She whistled to herself, rearranging things on the desk. "This will need tidying… I think we should have a silver and blue scheme this time."

"She's cracked," Estelle mouthed at the two of us.

"They don't belong together," Cass hissed. "There's a reason it didn't work out the first time around—"

"Don't start, Cass," said Aunt Adelaide. "I don't need any of your negativity interrupting my big day."

"Big… day?" I said.

"Of course," said Aunt Adelaide. "We've decided to redo our wedding vows here in the library. Today. That way it won't interfere with anybody's holiday plans."

"Not the library," Estelle said, in placating tones. "How about I call the registry and ask if we can book something for later this month? You don't even have a wedding dress—"

"There is nothing that magic cannot accomplish, dear. I taught you that."

And she sauntered away, humming a tune that sounded vaguely like *here comes the bride* under her breath.

Estelle slumped down next to the front desk. "She's completely addled. Why did Aunt Candace do this?"

"You think she'd really want her sister to remarry?" I asked. "Even she wouldn't go that far for a prank."

"Who even knows with her?" Cass shook her head. "Maybe Dad did have a change of heart, but he couldn't stand the library. It drove him loopy on a daily basis."

"They were always better apart than together," Estelle added. "Not to mention they've been seeing other people. Mum has, anyway. Dad is married to his job. There is *no* way she'd get back with him, not in this lifetime."

"Unless there was a love potion involved," Cass said. "I can brew an antidote..."

"It's not a love potion," I said. "Aunt Candace wrote this exact scenario into a book, right? It's another effect of the werewolf spell. Except instead of werewolves..."

"It's love stories," finished Estelle. "Yes, I know that, but Mum's going to regret it if she rushes through this wedding. And with the library's magic, she's perfectly capable of conjuring up everything she needs today. Wedding dresses, decorations..." She broke off as the shelves rumbled, folding backwards to clear a space on the carpet. "A dance floor, too."

"The spell's effects should stop at midnight," I said. "That's when the werewolves disappeared, right? Tomorrow is a different story, but we need to stall her until then."

"You're right." Estelle got to her feet, her usual composure sliding back into place. "She can't have lost all her common sense."

"Did you hear her?" Cass said. "She was *singing.* She didn't even notice the knights jousting in front of our doors, *and* she forgot to open the library. I'd say she's not our mother at all. She's been replaced by this weird clone."

Aunt Adelaide bounded into view. "You three will be bridesmaids, of course," she said. "What colour dress do you want, Rory?"

"I—" I broke off. "I already have plans today. So do Cass and Estelle, right? We won't be back until midnight. So, since we're all busy, we think you should wait until—"

"Really?" she asked. "Where are you going?"

"I'm seeing Xavier—"

She waved a hand. "Bring him with you. The whole town will be coming. I'm adding the finishing touches to the invitations, and I'll pay Zee generously to make us a wedding cake on short notice."

"The last I heard she was avoiding those horsemen," I said. "*They're* not coming, right?"

"I don't see why not." She sauntered away, a pleased smile on her face.

Estelle's composure cracked and she groaned. "Sorry, Rory. I'm with Cass—she's lost her mind."

At that moment, Aunt Candace wandered over from the living quarters, with Jet perched on her shoulder.

"Maurice is getting a divorce," she announced.

"And Aunt Adelaide is getting married," I informed her. "Today. Here in the library."

She blinked. "I don't follow you."

Cass scowled. "Aunt Candace, please tell me you're not under the spell, too. Our mother and father have suddenly put aside years of conflict because of the effect of a spell based on one of *your* books."

"*Fool Me Twice.* It's a second chance romance," she said, slapping her forehead. "Why didn't I see it before?"

"I'm glad we know the name of the book," Cass said caustically. "Can you tell us how to put a stop to it?"

"It's that Ursula Hancock," said Aunt Candace. "I should have known."

"Who?" I said blankly.

"Her 'friend'," Estelle said. "The one from university."

"The person she was spying on earlier," I added.

"Yes, her," she said. "She's here to write a story on the town for that ghastly paper of hers, and I'm sure she finds it very amusing to unleash chaos in order to give her story a bit of flavour."

"The spell started in here," I reminded her. "Has she even been near the library? Or read your books?"

"We were classmates at university," she said. "Of course she's read my books. She'd find the situation to her advantage, no doubt. I will speak with her."

"You'd better," Cass called after her. "I bet this friend of hers thinks she's as nuts as those bloody knights. I've never met anyone called Ursula Hancock. Her parents must have really hated her."

"Never mind that," I said. "If she's running a report on the town for her paper, she must have a serious grudge against Aunt Candace to do this. Who curses someone for a good story?"

"Aunt Candace would do it," said Cass.

"She's never gone this far," Estelle said. "She prefers to write chaos into her books, not actively participate in it. I don't know about this friend of hers, though."

"Not sure they're friends," I said. "I caught her trying to spy on her at the hotel, but a couple interrupted by starting an argument that ended in one of them being thrown out the window. I bet *that* came from one of her books, too."

Estelle groaned. "Maybe in the original book, the marriage gets called off?"

"Doubt we'll get that lucky," I said. "Not that I've read all her books, but she didn't literally base the characters on Aunt Adelaide and Elliot, right?"

Her brow crinkled. "Not that I know of. I don't know why the horsemen appeared and none of the other characters did."

"Unless that's where the werewolves ended up," Cass said. "And none of this is random. Someone targeted our family on purpose."

"They targeted Aunt Candace's books," I corrected. "She was supposed to be fetching her own copies to have a look at, but I'm guessing she got distracted by Jet's gossip. If a dozen books came to life at once, though—how are we supposed to know which started it?"

"We aren't," said Estelle. "It sounds like one spell got out of hand. It's not even a regular illusion spell, because they look *exactly* like the characters from the books. Aunt Candace isn't controlling the spell. I don't think even the person who set it off is, to be honest. All they have to do is let the story take over."

"Never mind how it happened," said Cass. "We have to stop this wedding."

I'd never heard Cass volunteering to work with the rest of us before, but there was a first time for everything.

"Well, you're the expert at getting the library to pull tricks on people," I said.

"Not her," she said. "We're not all as gullible as you are,

Rory. Our mother has better control over the library than the rest of us put together. If she wants to make the library host a wedding, there's nothing we can do to stop her. Unless we sabotage the wedding itself or stop Dad from showing up."

Estelle nodded slowly. "Okay. Cass, you're best at using the library to create diversions. As for me, I'll find Dad and see what *he* has to say about this. Rory..."

"I'll come with you." I didn't like the expression on Cass's face, and besides, I wouldn't want to get on Aunt Adelaide's bad side while she was neck-deep in wedding plans. I hoped Aunt Candace was able to talk sense into her... but hoping for common sense from someone who'd been wandering around trying to spy on her former classmate was probably too much to ask.

This isn't going to end well.

Once again, Estelle and I left the library. As we did so, Estelle waved her wand, conjuring a sign above the doors that read, *Closed.*

"That won't stop my mum from issuing wedding invitations," she said, "but at least it should stop anyone wandering into the library when she's in that state."

"Good," I said. "I hope people will be too busy with Christmas shopping to visit the library. Or too scared of being chased by a knight on horseback."

On cue, Zee from the bakery rode past on the back of a snow-white horse behind an armoured knight, leaving a trail of flour behind her.

"Oh, no," said Estelle.

I ran with her to the bakery to find the place covered in flour. Estelle pulled her wand out and gave it a wave, clearing the mess up in an instant.

"Useful spell," I said. "Wish I'd known that one when I was cleaning the rubbish out of the Reading Corner."

If I ever got my hands on a wand. At this rate, the town's citizens would all lose their collective minds before I ever had the chance to see if I could make it as a proper witch.

"It's not like Zee to run off in the middle of a workday," she said. "How are we supposed to stop everyone in town from making ridiculous decisions?"

There was a flash of light and a long piece of parchment appeared on the cash register. Estelle picked it up, her eyes widening. "My mother has put in an order for a wedding cake. And full catering. Does she not remember that Zee hasn't managed to find a new assistant yet?"

"Not to mention she isn't even here." But I suspected nothing would stop Aunt Adelaide when she was on a mission.

Estelle gasped, grabbing my arm. Outside, the air was thick with purple sparkles, sprinkling overhead like confetti. "What's she done now?"

We hurried outside as the confetti merged into purple scraps of paper, decorated with glittering sequins. Neon yellow text appeared on each piece of paper: *You are cordially invited to the wedding of Adelaide Hawthorn and Elliot Langley.*

"She's already sent out the invitations." Estelle sighed. "This is a disaster."

I looked around the square. Even the jousting had stopped as the knights reached up to catch the falling invitations in their hands. There were more scraps of paper than there were actual people in town. Nobody would be missed.

"Because we really need a bunch of knights at the wedding who think it's okay to harass women and steal flowers." Estelle rubbed her forehead. "I *have* to get Mum to call it off. If we catch my dad and talk him out of it, we'll still have to deal with all the publicity. But this… there's no way anyone will forget it, even if they're under a spell. We'll be the laughing stock of the town for months."

She's right. Everyone in town had seen the names. Aunt Adelaide, even if it never went ahead, would be mortified that the whole town would think she and her ex-husband had even considered reconciling.

Think, Rory. Invitations continued to fall from the sky, sticking to the damp paving stones. I reread the text. *Wedding invitation,* the title said. No ambiguity there. I took an invitation in hand, turning it over.

"What if I changed the date?" I suggested. "Remember how I changed the text of that cursed poem and undid the curse in the process? The invitations were created using biblio-witch magic, so if I change one invitation, the others will change, too."

"Good point." Estelle brightened. "If the wedding is postponed until later, then the spell will wear off before it gets to that point. But… but everyone will still think my mum and dad are getting married. They won't forget that."

"Then why not change the occasion?" Inspiration struck. "We can get the library to throw a Christmas party, right? You've done it before."

"I have," she said. "I'm surprised Mum hasn't roped me into helping—I'm supposed to be head of hospitality.

Then again, she barely knows her own name at the moment."

I pulled my biblio-witch pen from my pocket and pressed it against the piece of paper. Then I crossed out 'wedding' and put 'Christmas party', trying to copy the looping font. The ink shimmered, and then to my intense relief, it changed to match the font on the invitation.

Smiling, Estelle put her own wand away. "Perfect."

"They'll still show up expecting a party," I added. "But all we have to do is find a way to keep Aunt Adelaide and Elliot from finding out we changed the invitations, and the others will be none the wiser. Crisis averted."

"You're amazing." She wrapped her arms around me in a relieved hug.

"Not that we'll be able to stop the knights from showing up," I added. "I'd change the invitations to ban all knights from coming into the library, but I don't want to get on the bad side of men carrying sharp swords."

"Mum will handle them," she said. "I think. We can't stop people from making bad decisions… but we *could* put a spell on the guests so they don't suffer any bad effects from anything they do today."

"What, spike the drinks so everyone falls asleep and loses their memory of all the mistakes they made?" I said. "Can you do that?"

"Theoretically? Yes. I'll have to think about how to administer it…"

"The wedding cake?" I suggested. "Or—just offer everyone free champagne as they walk in. They do that at weddings, right?"

"You're a genius," she said. "I hope Cass has managed to come up with a distraction or three. I'll devise a way to keep Dad busy. Rory, can you tell Cass and Aunt Candace about the change of plans?"

"I will if I see them," I said. "Now all we have to do is keep your mother from contacting him until the wedding. Which is in…" I checked the time on the invitation. "Four hours."

Estelle groaned. "I'm going to need some genuine champagne before we start spiking it with a forgetfulness potion."

6

The party—or wedding—was underway. Upon returning to the library, I told Cass about my change of plans. While she wouldn't admit it, she seemed impressed with how I'd salvaged the situation.

Now all I had to do was not screw up in the next few hours. Of course, keeping Aunt Adelaide from seeing the altered invitations was a task and a half on its own. I had to bribe Sylvester to knock over a crate of books on the upper floor to keep her from intervening when the champagne showed up.

"I expect a raise for this," he called down at me.

"You don't even get paid. You're an owl." *Or does he?* I'd have to ask one of my aunts, assuming they didn't want to hide from the public eye forever when this was over.

"Mum will be annoyed that she spent so much of our budget on an unnecessary party," Estelle admitted.

"Bet she'll cheer when she finds out you knocked Dad out, though," Cass added.

"You did?" I turned to Estelle, raising my eyebrows.

"I caught him trying to hire a band to sing an hour-long epic about how amazing my mum is," she said. "I had to use a spell on him for his own safety. He won't remember."

"I don't see why you didn't just cancel the whole thing," said Cass. "The guests will still remember it all, and someone will work out what happened."

"Not when the champagne kicks in, they won't," Estelle said.

"You're not planning to poison the guests, are you?" Sylvester flew over our heads, clucking his beak in disapproval.

"No," I said. "We're planning to knock everyone out before they make any more mistakes under the influence of the spell. It's better that way. People do ridiculous things at parties *without* channelling Aunt Candace's romance novels."

"Exactly," said Estelle. "If we can't stop the party, then we can at least stop Mum from making an error she'll regret."

"Like us?" Cass said. "That's what you're saying? She regrets having us."

Estelle went pink. "Cass, I didn't mean that."

"Told you that, did she?" Cass's eyes narrowed. "Yeah, right."

"What's with her?" I frowned after her as she stormed off.

Estelle swore under her breath. "I should have known the stress would get to her."

That left it to the two of us to hold the fort alone. And Sylvester, who was far more amused and entertained by the situation than the rest of us.

"You still have tinsel all over the balconies, by the way," said the owl.

"Knew I forgot something." Estelle pulled out her wand. "We don't have to change all the decorations. I'll just tell Mum that Dad wanted a Christmas theme and she'll believe me. I mean, with the mood she's in at the moment, I could tell her he wanted murals of naked centaurs and she'd go along with it."

"See, now I know why you're head of hospitality," I said. "All I have to do is not poison the guests with that champagne. Are we using a potion?"

"Not to worry, I took care of it." Estelle waved her wand and a jug filled with clear liquid levitated over to the table set up on the right-hand side of the door, laden with champagne glasses. "I brought enough to go around. The worst that can happen is that it'll take too long to take effect, or some of their memories might linger anyway. But we can just tell them they went to a party and had a little too much to drink. No need to mention the spell."

"Sounds like a plan. I don't think anyone will complain about the decorating scheme." The library was unrecognisable, the bookshelves draped in shimmering purple curtains to protect their contents. Glittering tinsel twirled around the bannisters, and an array of floating purple balloons drifted up to the ceiling.

"Just as long as nobody damages the books." Estelle waved her wand, conjuring up 'no entry' signs for the door leading to our family's living quarters and the stairs to the upper levels. I watched her with a pang of regret that I didn't have a wand of my own to help out.

Pushing the feeling aside, I moved to the table with the champagne glasses and set about distributing the potion among the glasses, using the real champagne to hide the clear liquid from view. "Have you tested this on anyone, Estelle? We don't want everyone turning into frogs."

"Some of us would find it amusing," Sylvester put in, poking a balloon with his claw.

"Quit that." Estelle shooed him away and came to help me. "I'll test it on Sylvester."

"You won't." He flew out of reach. "If you do, I will leave here, never to return."

"Melodramatic, much?" Estelle put down the jug. "Okay, who wants to play lab rat?"

"I would, but one of us has to keep an eye on—" I broke off as Aunt Adelaide drifted over. "Oh, hey, Aunt Adelaide."

"Oh, there you are, Mum," said Estelle. "I decided to go for a Christmas theme—obvious reasons."

"Perfect," said Aunt Adelaide. "Where's Cass?"

"She's a little freaked out by the whole thing," said Estelle. "Since you and Dad have been apart for so long. I'm sure she'll show up when the wedding starts."

Aunt Adelaide halted beside us. To my alarm, her eyes were swimming with tears. "I'm sorry for what the divorce did to you. You must have felt so upset when your father had to leave the library."

"It didn't do any harm," Estelle insisted. "It's fine."

"Doesn't everyone cry at their wedding?" She sniffed. "Granted, I've done this before, and I don't remember it being quite so…"

Is she having regrets? If she called off the wedding, we'd have some explaining to do to the townspeople, considering they all thought we were hosting a Christmas party.

"I've never married, so I don't know," I said carefully.

"Right, you're young." She sniffed. "Both of you. You have your whole lives ahead of you. You don't have to repeat my mistakes."

Estelle cleared her throat. "Uh, Mum, there's not long to go until you have to greet the guests. Are you going to change into your wedding dress?"

She blew her nose. "Yes, I'm pulling myself together."

I felt a pang as she turned away. Were some of her feelings real after all? *Real or not, any decision made under the influence of a spell is worth putting on hold.*

"I'm going to be serving champagne on the door." Estelle offered her a glass. "Want to try some? For courage?"

"I shouldn't," she said. "But now you mention it, I *am* nervous. Thank you, Estelle."

She drank the champagne in one go, then handed the glass back to her.

"Interesting taste," she said.

"It's a new recipe," Estelle said. "You should go and change into your dress."

"Yes, I will do that... thank you." Aunt Adelaide walked off in a daze.

"How long?" I mouthed to Estelle.

"Less than half an hour," she said in an undertone. "That gives us enough time to set the place up ready for the party, while pretending things are going ahead as normal."

Hmm. Aunt Candace was noticeably absent, too. With trepidation, I ducked under the 'do not enter' sign to our living quarters. In the sitting room, Aunt Candace sat surrounded by a stack of her own paperbacks, looking satisfied with herself. "I knew I left these somewhere."

"You know there's a party about to start, don't you?" I said. "Your sister's 'wedding'?"

"Yes, I know, I know." She waved an impatient hand. "She'll forgive me. One wedding is quite enough for a lifetime. I thought you needed me to fetch these books."

"Later." I winced, hearing the doorbell. "The guests are here. Can you please give me a hand with them and go back to the books later?"

I hurried into the lobby and skidded to a halt on the dance floor. *Oh, no.* Three horsemen stood in the entryway, looking around at the balloons and tinsel-clad bookshelves and clutching purple invitations in their hands. They must have picked up invitations between jousting and seducing the town's citizens.

"Champagne?" Cass called to the guests, herding them over to the table.

Thank you, Cass. While she wore her customary scowl, she hadn't disappeared after all. Shooting her a grateful look, I went to join her.

"I'm told this is a momentous occasion," said the knight, taking the glass from her. "But where are the other guests?"

"My aunt isn't feeling well," I said, "so she sent me to welcome you all. Help yourselves to champagne, but remember to leave some for the other guests."

Estelle moved in behind me, starting her hostess speech. The bride was conspicuously absent, but the guests wouldn't notice when the champagne kicked in.

Soon enough, the other guests began to stream into the library in groups. Witches, werewolves, elves, even the odd vampire or two—everyone in town had heard about the party. Thanking my lucky stars that we'd managed to avert total catastrophe, I joined Cass in handing out glasses of champagne, while Sylvester swooped overhead, wearing a halo of tinsel on his head and apparently enjoying the festivities. Aunt Candace, unsurprisingly, was nowhere to be seen.

An hour into the night, I'd almost started to enjoy myself. In a lull between guest arrivals, Estelle ran past the champagne table, looking frazzled. "One of the knights just challenged someone to a duel. At least I'm used to dealing with punch-ups over the textbooks."

"Need any help?" I called after her, spotting a bunch of new arrivals surge in. I grabbed some more champagne glasses to hand out, and my heart flipped over. Xavier walked in, looking at the gathered guests as though unsure how he'd ended up here. Then he set eyes on me.

"Oh, hey." Heat crept up my neck. He was wearing his usual dark clothing, yet he still didn't look out of place. "Come to enjoy the party?"

"What's the occasion?" he asked. "And why is there a wedding cake over there?"

"Oh, no." I handed the glass to the green-hatted witch who'd just walked in and hastened over to the table with the wedding cake on it—thankfully hidden out of sight behind the champagne. "My Aunt Adelaide fell under the effects of the curse and organised this big event, so we're trying to stop it from being as much of a disaster as it could have been."

"Wait, so nobody's getting married?" He stepped aside as I wheeled the cake table out of sight behind the bookcases.

"My aunt decided to get remarried on a whim, so we changed the invitations so they told everyone it was a

Christmas party," I explained. "In about half an hour, all the guests will fall unconscious, so don't drink the champagne."

His eyes grew wide. "Wow, you put this together fast."

"Aunt Adelaide set the whole thing up. I just changed the invitations so they said it was a Christmas party, spiked the drinks, and now I'm trying to go ahead as though this was supposed to happen all along."

"It's impressive," he commented. "I'm sure your aunt will thank you for it."

Estelle ran over and transformed the wedding cake into a chocolate log with one wave of her wand.

"Thanks." I released a sigh of relief, moving towards the dance floor. "I'd avoid Aunt Adelaide for the rest of the week, mind."

He chuckled. "I'm still impressed by how you handled the situation, considering how little time you had to prepare."

"So am I, to be honest." Stopping a minor disaster from turning into a major one was achievement enough. But the guests seemed to be having a genuinely good time. Even Cass had managed to hold back from making any caustic remarks, while the knights had stopped trying to yank people onto their horses and occupied the dance floor, armour and all. For the first time since that morning, I felt myself begin to relax.

"Of course," Xavier said, in answer. "Why would you doubt it?"

"This is the first time I've had to deal with Aunt Adelaide being the person causing a scene," I said. "I suppose I should be relieved that the account of my own life story didn't come to life as well."

Xavier's brows rose. "Your aunt wrote a book about you?"

"She wrote the story of how my parents met," I explained. "I know the story, of course, but not Aunt Candace's version."

"Really?" he said. "I don't think you've told me about it before."

"I reckon she made the tale more dramatic than it actually was." I stepped closer to him as one of the knights staggered past, dropping flowers everywhere. "Dad always said he met Mum on the train when he was away on business, and fell head over heels the instant he set eyes on her. Then he left the magical world behind to be with her. When she died… he was broken. We both were." I sucked in a painful breath, realising that this was the first time I'd told the story aloud to anyone. "But he put himself back together for my sake, and we—we were a family. He still never came back to the magical world, though. He didn't even have a wand or anything at home. I guess he worried I'd find it and learn the truth. If he wanted to stay with my mum, he had to give up magic forever. The rules are strict on that."

"That's a pity," he said. "I'm glad you were able to find your own way here, though, Rory."

"Sorry, it's kind of a sad story for a party," I said. "I guess you know all about rules, huh. Is your boss okay with you being here?"

"We never got to finish our date yesterday," he said, disregarding my question. "I hoped you might dance with me, at least."

Ack. Is he under the spell? I really couldn't tell. In the lights of the dance floor, with music playing in the background, I felt like I'd imbibed more genuine champagne than was wise. "Uh, don't take this the wrong way, but people are making... questionable decisions today. If it's anything like yesterday, the effects won't fade until midnight."

"You don't want to dance with me?" He stepped back, giving me the chance to tell him to leave.

But I did want to—so badly that it startled me. Whether he was under the effects of the spell or not, his words made tingles race up my spine. And my own feelings were clear enough. Perhaps that's why the spell hadn't affected me.

"Okay," I said. "Sure, I will."

The dance floor filled most of the lobby, so all we had to do was move to the music. Considering Xavier had hinted that his Reaper powers gave him unnatural athletic abilities, it made sense that he'd be a good dancer. I was starting to feel a little crazy. Maybe I'd fallen under the spell after all, because being with Xavier made me want in a way I never had before.

I smiled up at him and he smiled back. *This is real. It's all real.*

Drops of snow rained down on us. I looked up and caught one on my tongue. Xavier did, too, leaning closer to me. My heart pounded, but he... didn't have a heartbeat.

The realisation made me hesitate. Even if I didn't regret this experience, he might, if it had consequences for his position as Reaper.

"Xavier, what would your boss have to say about... this?" I gestured between us.

"This what?"

"You know," I said awkwardly. "You. And me."

Please tell me I didn't misread the situation. Please. "I don't plan on telling him," he said. "My boss has never taken an interest in my life outside of my job, and I don't expect him to start now."

That's no answer. If it's forbidden, then I'd rather be forewarned. He wasn't even allowed a mobile phone. He also didn't age and was a lot older than me, for all I knew. Then again, that was something he'd have brought up already if it was going to be an issue, right?

Another snowflake landed on my tongue, fizzling out. It tasted of champagne.

Uh-oh.

Then Xavier's scent invaded my space. I wouldn't have expected the Reaper to have a particular smell, but he did —chilly as moonlight on water, and utterly intoxicating. My face heated as he cupped my chin, my head spinning pleasantly. More droplets fell on my face and I smiled, tasting them on my tongue. He leaned his head closer, brushing his lips over mine, and I gasped in surprise.

Then he spun me around, startling a laugh from me. I let him twirl me on the spot and gave myself entirely to the rhythm. I couldn't remember the last time I'd metaphorically let my hair down, and all my misgivings melted away with the snow-champagne raining down on the crowd.

I was dancing with the Reaper, and every inch of me was on fire.

A thump brought me back to reality as the couple beside us sank to the ground in a dead faint. Two more couples followed. In seconds, unconscious dancers lay sprawled on the dance floor. Looked like the effects of the champagne were kicking in. I spun to a halt, leaning on Xavier for balance. "Whoa."

"You okay, Rory?" he said.

My heartbeat drummed in my ears. "You should know about the champagne—"

The door flew open, a torrent of darkness dispelling all the bright party lights. The guests collectively gasped, and several others fainted, joining their companions on the floor.

The Grim Reaper stood in the doorway, his shadowy eyes roving over the decorations, the dancing—or unconscious—crowd, and in the middle of it all, Xavier, who stood stock-still as though he'd been punched.

The tall, shadowy man beckoned to Xavier and me. "Come."

The crowd parted to let Xavier through. My heart skittered, and the dizzying effect of the spell vanished as though someone had dumped a bucket of icy water over my head.

Oh, god. I should have given him the champagne after all. Better an unconscious Reaper than a Reaper dancing with a mortal in public.

The Grim Reaper glided out the doors, more of a shadow than a person. Icy air blew in from outside, made a thousand times colder by the Reaper's presence. His shadowy form seemed to suck out all the lights, from the glittering tinsel to the balloons floating above the crowd. The library's noise and comfortable warmth vanished as the Reaper beckoned Xavier into the night.

"There is a soul in need of assistance," he said, his voice echoing. "And here I find you canoodling with mortals, Xavier. I thought you knew to leave all mortal pursuits behind when you took on your apprenticeship with me."

"My apologies." Xavier's voice didn't shake, which was impressive. "I received an invitation to the party and it didn't cross my mind that I would be unable to detect any souls passing on while I was in there."

Might that be another side effect of the spell? It was a surprise that it affected Reapers at all, considering they were supposed to be outside the same world as the rest of us.

The Reaper's eyes slid to mine, and I fought the instinct to hide. My heart beat erratically, while my head spun as though I was drunk for real. Apologies rose to my tongue, quelled when his icy blue gaze looked into my soul. I couldn't move. I could hardly breathe.

"Relationships with mortals are forbidden," he said. "I thought you knew the rules, Xavier."

"He's under a spell," I blurted. "We all are."

"You put him under your spell?"

"No!" I said hastily. "It's—everyone in town is under the same spell. They're making out-of-character decisions and pursuing romances with people who they wouldn't normally spend time with. That's why I had to throw the party—I had to find a way to give everyone a potion that undid the spell before anyone got hurt."

"Then why has it not worn off my apprentice yet?" he said. "I do not think you are being entirely truthful with me, Aurora Hawthorn."

No, but if I admit I have a crush on your apprentice, you'll probably reap my soul.

"Ask my aunt, when she wakes up." My head gave

another lurch, and I wondered if I might throw up. "The effects of the antidote are coming on..."

"What are you talking about?" He didn't believe me. Not only that, he thought *I'd* seduced Xavier into breaking the rules.

"Come with me," he said, and Xavier stepped off the doorstep without looking back.

I tried to tell him that Xavier hadn't done anything wrong., but my head was spinning, and I dropped to my knees. Then blackness descended in a wave, sweeping me away.

7

It was with great relief that I walked downstairs the following morning to find all signs of the party had vanished. Aside from the Christmas decorations, which remained in place, there were no guests napping on the floor or discarded champagne glasses, nor any knights —in or out of armour. Someone must have carried me to bed, because the last thing I remembered was passing out on the doorstep. After Xavier and I… *oh, no.*

My cheeks burned, my whole body shrivelling with embarrassment. What was I thinking? Xavier would never have pursued me in that manner if he hadn't been under the spell, but I had no such excuse. And what if the Grim Reaper had punished Xavier for neglecting his duties?

Cass walked out of the living room, looking almost cheerful.

"Oh, you're up," she said. "My mum left us some coffee, so I assume she's back to normal."

"Good." At least one thing had gone right. "Uh, what happened last night? How'd everyone get home?"

"You slept through the whole thing," Cass answered. "By the time the Reaper left, most of the guests were unconscious. Estelle and I cleaned up, and at midnight, most of them woke up. We told them they fell asleep at the party and helped them on their way home. Most of them were still groggy, so there's no harm done."

"And who brought me inside?" I walked into the kitchen, gratefully picking up a steaming mug of coffee. My Aunt Adelaide was back—and unmarried. *Thank god for that.*

"Estelle did," she said. "You were lying on the doorstep, totally out cold. Anyway, Mum woke up at midnight and figured out what was going on. She helped us clear up."

"Where did those knights on horseback go?" I sipped my coffee.

"They all ran away when the Reaper showed up," she said. "You know, most people respect him. I can't believe you're scared of harmless old vampires and not the angel of death."

"I *am* scared of him. I didn't know he was so mortally offended by weddings or parties."

The Grim Reaper had scared me half to death, but because I liked Xavier too much, a not-insignificant part of me had been willing to risk the Reaper's wrath last night. Whatever that said about me, a discussion of my non-existent love life with Cass was the last thing I needed right now.

She gave me a pitying look. "Did you seriously need to pretend to be under a spell to take that next step with Xavier?"

We're doing this now? "He *was* under the spell," I told her. "There's nothing between us. And if I'd tried anything last night, I would have been taking advantage."

It was unfair to Xavier that I'd escaped with no punishment other than my guilty conscience and an eternity of embarrassment, and I hoped the Grim Reaper had realised that if not for the spell, Xavier would never have behaved the way he had. For both our sakes.

"Whatever you say," said Cass. "Estelle—there you are."

Estelle came into the kitchen, yawning. "Oh, good, you're awake, Rory. You worried me when you passed out on the doorstep."

"I guess the effects of that champagne came on hard." I took a seat at the kitchen table and drank more coffee. "Does your mother remember what she did while under the spell?"

"Some of it," Estelle said. "I told her the rest. But Dad doesn't remember a thing, so I decided to leave him be. It's better that way."

Cass's mouth thinned. "So that's it? We just carry on as though nothing happened?"

"Cass, you know perfectly well that it would have been an utter disaster if we'd let that wedding go ahead as planned," said Estelle. "Dad *hates* the library. He can't stand parties either."

"Did he live here the whole time they were married?" I asked.

"Yes," said Estelle. "That's why he thinks it's a madhouse. In fairness, the library took a dislike to him, and so did Sylvester."

"That's putting it mildly," Cass said, in sour tones.

"So why did the spell affect her and not us?" I wondered aloud. It hadn't affected Aunt Candace either, but then again, the books *were* hers. Perhaps that granted her some degree of immunity.

"Are you sure it didn't affect you?" Cass snorted. "If the way you kept drooling over the Reaper wasn't an act, you might as well let him bury you now."

"Cass," said Estelle. "I know you're upset about Mum and Dad—"

"Are you kidding? They'd have set the library on fire by the week's end if the wedding had gone ahead." She rolled her eyes. "I'm angry with the person who set off this blasted curse, but I think we dealt with it just fine."

"That's what I mean," I said. "It hit your mum and not the rest of us. If it's a curse, it usually has an intended target, right?"

"You mean it's aimed at our mum?" Estelle frowned. "No, if anything, you'd think the target would be Aunt Candace. But she didn't fall under the spell's effects at all."

"Exactly," I said. "Do we know anyone who holds enough of a grudge against our family that they'd turn her books against us?"

"Never mind that," said Cass. "Which book is it today? It'd be a fine thing if her horror pen name kicked in on Christmas. The whole town would blacklist us for life."

"She has a horror pen name?" I looked at Estelle in alarm.

"If the curse is still on, then... yes, that could happen." Her brow furrowed. "She has five pen names that we know of. The spell might be cycling through each name, one per day, or moving around at random."

"It started with the werewolf book, though," I said. "Aunt Candace brought a stack of her own books downstairs yesterday. They're in the living room."

"I doubt the person who did this broke into her private quarters," said Cass. "The last person who went in there ended up dead. I mean, deader than dead."

"Cass!" Estelle said sharply. "Dominic has nothing to do with this. There's no need to be mean."

I grimaced at the memory of Aunt Candace's vampire ex-boyfriend, who'd been murdered by a deranged killer who'd targeted my family. This time, I wouldn't be making any misplaced accusations, but there was something downright weird about someone using a spell rooted in Aunt Candace's books to mess with us. It felt more like a personal grudge than a random prank.

"Whoever did it, if it's a curse, only the caster can undo it." I'd learned that lesson early on in the magical world and had never forgotten.

"True," said Estelle. "I think we should ask an expert."

"You mean the curse-breaker," I said.

Mr Bennet, the local curse-breaker, was not the biggest fan of our family. He'd accused Grandma of practising dark magic when she'd created the library, and while he'd apologised for his attitude towards me the week I'd moved to town, I wasn't keen to pay him another visit.

Still, I'd feel more useful going into town to get answers than hanging around the library lamenting what an utter fool I'd made of myself last night.

"I'm not talking to him," Cass said.

"Fine," Estelle responded. "Rory and I will. You and Mum can open the library. And if she's run off under the effects of a spell again, you can figure out how to deal with it this time."

Once we'd grabbed some breakfast, Estelle and I

headed out into the town square. It was yet another cold, windy day, and discarded flowers littered the square—thankfully, without their owners.

"At least the horses are gone," Estelle said. "Poor Harold. Half his flower display is missing."

The wererabbit marched around the square gathering up blooms. "Bloody menaces," he growled. "Those knights paid me in solid gold coins. Every one of them vanished at midnight."

"What, the coins as well as the knights?" Uh-oh. Everything they carried must have been a creation of the spell, too.

"Here, let me help you," said Estelle, waving her wand at the heaps of flowers so they rearranged themselves in neat rows.

Harold grunted thanks and resumed collecting discarded petals.

"Poor guy," Estelle said in an undertone. "I guess a lot of people are going to be cleaning up the aftermath. At least the library is still in one piece."

We made our way to the curse-breaker's small shop on the seafront. Inside, the tall, thin man behind the counter wore his customary scowl.

"Oh," Mr Bennet said. "It's you."

"You didn't come to the party?" I didn't need to ask. Even if he'd fallen under the influence of the curse, his dislike of the library remained intact. He didn't look like the type of person who liked parties even if my family wasn't involved.

"No," he said. "What made your aunt call off the wedding?"

Estelle stiffened at my side. "Uh, excuse me?"

"I saw the invitations change," he said. "I'm familiar with the way your magic works. Someone altered the text on the invitations and hoped nobody would notice."

Ack. "That's actually what we want to talk to you about," I improvised. "My aunt and her ex-husband were cursed into falling in love with one another. The same curse has been affecting people all over town. I changed the wedding invitations so my aunt and her ex-husband wouldn't have any regrets when the effects wore off."

His brows crept higher and higher as I described the effects of the curse and how they'd changed from conjuring up werewolves to inciting wedding planning.

"What is the curse doing today, then?" he asked.

"Nothing so far," I said. "But it didn't stop after one day. That's what led us to conclude it's a curse and not a spell, and it seems to be based on our aunt's books. Is that even possible?"

He leaned over the counter. "If I hadn't heard so many outlandish stories of people acting the fool yesterday, I'd disbelieve it," he said. "As it is... your aunt may have encountered a Manifestation Curse."

"What's that?" asked Estelle.

"Essentially, it makes the imaginary real," said Mr Bennet. "And once used, it will hop between targets, bringing them to life over and over again until it runs its course. For it to have lasted more than a day, it must be a very strong curse."

"How would someone go about creating a curse like that?" I asked.

"Very tricky magic," he answered. "I imagine your library contains instructions on how to create one."

Estelle flushed. "We've been monitoring any use of the

curses section, and nobody has checked out our guides to advanced curses all month."

"Then someone from your own family did it," he said, without batting an eyelid. "It wouldn't be the first time."

"I wouldn't make accusations against our family, Mr Bennet," Estelle said tightly. "Aunt Candace wouldn't curse any of us. I assume someone thought it would be a fun prank to play on our family, but the consequences have the potential to affect the whole town."

I didn't believe Aunt Candace was responsible for yesterday's catastrophe either. The only person she seemed to suspect of wrongdoing was this Ursula Hancock, but we couldn't go around making accusations without proof. Aunt Candace's ex-schoolmate hadn't even been in the library when the curse had kicked off. As far as I knew, she hadn't come to the party, either.

"How long can that type of curse last?" I asked.

"Any length of time, depending on its strength," he said. "I believe the record is several months."

Months? We couldn't deal with months of knights on horseback and unexpected weddings. Sooner or later, someone would realise the source of the chaos came from the library. I didn't want to imagine what might happen to my home if the magical authorities found out.

"Don't look so despairing," said Mr Bennet. "Find the source of the curse. It shouldn't be that difficult."

"The source—meaning the book?" I struggled to keep my voice even.

"What else?" He waved a hand. "Given yesterday's events, you'll want to handle the curse sooner rather than later. Good day."

Nothing to do but head back to the library. At least

Aunt Candace had gathered all her books and stacked them in the living room. Once we'd found the book, we could look for a solution.

"At least he gave us a clue this time," I said to Estelle as we left the shop. "The book that started it. *The Adventures of Werewolves in Cyberland.* We should have had a closer look at the ones in the living room."

"I'm not sure it's one of them," Estelle said. "Those aren't the only copies of the books in existence, and it's possible that the curse was used *outside* of the library. The curse targeted the text in the books, not us."

"Then why did those werewolves appear inside the library first?" If the culprit had wanted to wreak havoc on the town, there were thousands of books they might have targeted. "It feels like they wanted our family to experience the brunt of the curse, otherwise they'd have picked a different book. They must have known Aunt Candace's alias, too. One of them, at least."

"You're right," she said. "I'd say we speak to the police and get a second opinion."

"Fair point. I didn't see Edwin at the party yesterday, but I suppose he was breaking up fights all day." Not just in the Christmas sales, but romantic spats, too. I hoped the champagne had undone the worst of the damage.

The police station looked much the same as ever, on the outside at least. Inside, however, the front desk was piled high with papers, while the wall on the right was covered in photographs and sketches of a tall man with a whiskery face, wearing various disguises.

Edwin turned to us in the middle of affixing another photograph to the wall. "Ah, Rory," he said. "Have you asked your aunt yet?"

"Asked her what?" I racked my brains, but I was pretty sure I hadn't even seen him yesterday. *Please tell me he didn't hear about the party.*

"For her autograph, of course."

"Oh." Had yesterday's shenanigans—Grim Reaper and all—entirely slipped his notice? "Um, I don't know if you heard, but there was a party at the library last night. It kept us busy all day, so I didn't have the chance to ask my aunt."

"Yes, I heard about the party," said Edwin. "I was preoccupied with hunting down our elusive thief. He stole a considerable sum of money from the bank last night."

"Oh, no." I'd bet the Magpie had taken advantage of everyone being at the party to go on a thieving spree. "Have you still not caught him yet?"

The elf scowled. "No. The thief leaves no clues before he strikes. I gather he enjoys the act of stealing more than he actually needs what he steals. That's why he's managed to avoid the authorities so far—his movements are unpredictable."

"But he's staying somewhere in town?" I thought of the chaos at the hotel yesterday. Everyone had been so distracted that the thief could have stolen the giant Christmas tree from the pier and it would still have taken hours for anyone to notice it was missing.

"So it would seem." He narrowed his eyes at the blurry photographs. I hadn't seen what a magical camera looked like, but the photos I'd seen had appeared clearer and more detailed than those from the normal world. Like a HD camera had captured every molecule. The distorted, unclear nature of the photos on the wall told me they'd been brought in from the normal world. "You didn't come to talk to me about the Magpie, did you? What is it?"

"The party," I said. "It wasn't… exactly planned."

"Oh, this party." He produced an invitation from underneath a stack of papers on the desk. "What was the occasion?"

"I don't know if you noticed," I said, "but someone seems to have cursed Aunt Candace's books as a prank. Yesterday, it was her romance novels. The day before, it was those werewolves… that's where they came from."

"So *that's* why they disappeared from their cells," he said. "And it also explains why my secretary had an unexpected affair with one of my troll guards."

Oh, no. How many relationships had been soured because of the effects of the curse? Also, Edwin must be fixated on the thief if he'd hardy noticed any of his employees were acting out of character.

"We're looking for the source of the curse," Estelle explained. "So far we've worked out that the person who cast it didn't use one of our reference books to do it. So they were either an expert on curses or they came from outside town."

Hmm. How many people in Ivory Beach were curse experts? Or was Aunt Candace's paranoia about her old friend not unwarranted after all? With no other obvious suspects, I was drawing a blank.

Edwin ran a hand through his sparse hair, his shoulders sagging with weariness. "I'm afraid I must concentrate my attention on apprehending this criminal. Most of the town was at your library last night and he still slipped our notice. The magpie symbol at the scene… it's my belief that the thief is using a disguise."

"What, like a spell?" Nobody I'd seen at the library had struck me as suspicious, but I hadn't been on the lookout for potential thieves. The entire town had been behaving out of character yesterday, even those of us who hadn't fallen directly under the curse. For all I knew, the thief had hidden among the knights on horseback.

"Perhaps," he said. "As for this curse of yours, you'll have to give me more information before I can apprehend the culprit. If you learn anything, feel free to let me know."

And that was that. Estelle and I left the police station behind and made our way back to the library.

"I guess he's under a lot of pressure," Estelle said. "I can't believe he didn't notice the party."

"Even the thief did," I said. "If this sort of thing keeps happening, we'll be overrun by criminal elements. At least the library looks normal today—"

As Estelle pushed the library doors open, I stepped over the threshold and abruptly flew into the air. Hands flailing, I floated on the spot, grabbing my Biblio-Witch Inventory. Estelle floated horizontally beside me, her eyes wide and her hair flying around her head.

"Where did gravity go?" I flipped the right way up. My head rushed with vertigo and I grabbed the desk for balance. A mistake—even the desk was floating, along with everything on it. I snatched up the logbook before it floated away into the maze of hovering shelves. *So much for normal.*

Aunt Adelaide floated across the ground floor, pursued by an irritated-looking Cass.

"Mum, what in the world is going on?" Estelle asked.

"It appears," said Aunt Adelaide, "that gravity has

stopped functioning. If I'm to guess, it's because most of my sister's sci-fi novels are set on spaceships or in zero-gravity environments."

"Great," said Cass. "Next bug-eyed aliens will be crawling out the walls."

"She's right," Estelle said. "That actually happened in two of her books. I dread to think what might have spawned on the third floor."

Cass swore. "If that curse has hurt any of my animals, I'll kill her."

She made for the stairs and flew several feet into the air, doing an interesting pirouette-like move I would never have thought I'd see Cass do. I held my breath as she leap-frogged around the lobby. Estelle gave a stifled giggle, then both of us collapsed into laughter. It was a relief, after such a frustrating week, to laugh hysterically at Cass's antics. Cass would make us pay for mocking her later, but right now, I didn't care.

"The curse can't be outside the library this time." I caught my breath. "We didn't start floating until we stepped inside."

"No, this must be the space station," said Estelle, her eyes sparkling with mirth. "I'll have to reread the series to find out what else we might run into."

"Never thought I'd say this, but we don't have time for reading," I said.

"She's right," said Aunt Adelaide. "Did you learn anything from the curse-breaker?"

"He thinks it's a Manifestation curse, whatever that is," I said. "Cast on one of Aunt Candace's books. But he said the information on *how* to use the curse was either from in here, or from outside town. And we already know nobody has been looking up curses in the last month."

"Outside town?" echoed Aunt Adelaide. "Why would anyone come here just to put a curse on our family?"

Cass gave up trying to climb the stairs and floated back to Aunt Adelaide's side. "I take it we're not opening the library today? Because bug-eyed aliens are a lot less appealing than the sexy naked werewolves."

Estelle choked on a laugh. "I think we should leave the place closed and say it's because we're recovering from the party. I don't want to be held responsible if someone gets eaten by an alien."

"If anything, they're more likely to be eaten by a manticore," I said. "Speaking of—is *everything* that isn't nailed to the floor floating in the air?"

"Yes," said Aunt Adelaide. "Even the books."

Uh-oh. "We'll keep the place closed, then," said Estelle. "Pretend we're taking a break until the new year. Everyone in town is suffering from memory loss and mild hangovers today, anyway."

"Even Edwin?" asked Aunt Adelaide.

"Not him," I said. "He's more concerned with the thief. The Magpie robbed the bank while everyone was at the party."

Aunt Adelaide muttered something unpleasant under her breath. "Well, that's not our business. *Where* Candace is hiding… oh, she did leave her books all over the living room. Have any of you looked in there for the source of the spell?"

"We'll have a look," Estelle said. "And we can fetch Aunt Candace, too. She's probably spying on that Ursula Hancock again."

"Maybe it *was* her," I said. "Assuming we believe what Mr Bennet said about the culprit being from outside town."

Cass made a derisive noise. "Since when have any of Aunt Candace's paranoid theories ever led to any meaningful conclusions?"

"The curse was put on one of her books, Cass," said Estelle. "How many people outside our family even knew she wrote under more than one pen name?"

"Good point," I said. "Though they might have only meant to target the one book and then the curse spread by itself. From what the curse-breaker said, that's possible. Would they need to pick up the book to put the curse on it?"

"Yes," said Estelle. "You know, we should have gone looking for that book from the start."

"Good luck finding it in here." Cass waved a hand at the floating shelves. "Even Sylvester will have trouble locating anything. Where is he, anyway?"

"Maybe he's tailing Aunt Candace again." Or hiding in the forbidden room until the chaos calmed down. Speaking of which—I should have consulted that room when I'd had the chance, because it was anyone's guess as to where the book of questions had disappeared to.

"Is there another way to summon the right book to hand?" I asked Estelle. Then something else hit me. "Wait, if the book came from outside the library, wouldn't it have automatically been shelved in the right place?"

Her expression sharpened. "That means it *must* be with the rest of Aunt Candace's books, assuming they're still all over the living room."

"They are," said Aunt Adelaide. "Floating, but in the

right place."

Estelle groaned. "We'll sort them out."

The instant we moved across the lobby, we began to drift into the air. Never mind the stairs—all we had to do was try to walk forwards and the momentum would carry us up four floors to the ceiling. "Maybe we'll find the missing upper corridor."

"Or get stuck in it." Estelle caught my hand, tugging me back to earth. With her free hand, she clung onto the door frame. "Mind your head."

"Ow." My forehead bounced off the edge of the door frame, but I floated into the corridor to the living quarters. Several more collisions later and we reached the living room, and were surrounded on all sides by floating books.

I picked up book after book, discarding the unfamiliar ones. A book titled *Entranced by the Normal: An Epic Paranormal-Normal Romance* caught my attention—the story of my dad's meeting with my mum. I still hadn't read it, but at this rate, I wouldn't have time for any reading for pleasure until the curse was gone.

A book with a metallic-coloured cover floated past and I grabbed it by my fingertips. *The Adventures of Werewolves in Cyberland.*

"Gotcha." I tucked it under my arm triumphantly. "Is this the only copy?"

"It's the only one I can see," said Estelle.

I opened the book to the front page and found a sprawling signature—Aunt Candace's, signed as her pen name.

"It's signed," I said. "And—the person it's signed to is Ursula Hancock."

8

"So it *is* her?" Estelle read the signature over my shoulder. "Is this definitely the book that kicked it off?"

"It's the only copy of *The Adventures of Werewolves in Cyberland* I can find in here." And Aunt Candace had personally gifted it to Ursula, according to the signature.

"Then Aunt Candace must have seen it," said Estelle. "Maybe that's where she is—confronting Ursula."

"Maybe, but why leave the book behind?" Something didn't add up. "Unless she forgot. Or couldn't be bothered to look through all these floating titles." *That* wasn't out of character for Aunt Candace. For someone who was a meticulous plotter, she wasn't known for thinking her actions through in the real world.

Estelle made a sceptical noise. "Unless she wanted to frame her, but that sounds a bit much even for Aunt Candace. We'll talk to her before we go to the police. I'd rather she didn't get arrested again, and I think Edwin would, too."

"Edwin doesn't seem to be paying close attention to anything other than that runaway thief," I said. "I doubt Aunt Candace is framing her ex-schoolmate, anyway. She'd have been a lot more blatant if she was."

"Still." Estelle hovered on the spot. "We'll talk to Ursula, but if it's not her…"

"What are you two talking about?" asked Aunt Adelaide.

"This." I held up the book. "It's signed to Ursula Hancock. Does the Manifestation Curse have to be cast directly onto its target to work, or can it work by proxy?"

Her gaze fixed on the book. "No. If that's the book the curse was initially used on, then the caster must be the one to remove it. That does not, however, mean the curse was cast in the library."

"So it may have been planted in here for us to find?" I guessed. "The only way to know for sure is to ask Aunt Candace. And Ursula, come to that."

"Do that," said Aunt Adelaide, with none of her usual warmth. "I'm intending to research the subject in more depth, assuming the books are still in the right sections."

She strode away, her coat swirling in the gravity-free air.

I stared after her for a moment. "She's not taking what happened yesterday well, is she?"

Estelle shook her head. "I think we should leave her alone for a while."

Once we'd floated through the library's oak doors, gravity came back, depositing both of us on the doorstep.

"Ow." Estelle's knees buckled, same as mine. "At least it's just the library this time around."

"Don't speak too soon," I said. "For all we know,

Ursula has been replaced by a space alien. Or Aunt Candace."

She groaned. "It was bad enough how my mum was acting yesterday. If it *was* Ursula who did this, I hope Aunt Candace curses her in return."

Estelle strode in the lead, absent of her usual cheer. I didn't blame her. It'd be a fine Christmas if everyone was at odds thanks to this curse.

"Have you seen Xavier?" she asked. "After last night, I mean? I can't believe the Reaper showed up at our doors. He's never done that before."

"He's not one for partying." Xavier was a different story. The memory of us dancing under the lights felt like someone else's, like it didn't belong to me at all. "No, I haven't seen Xavier. I guess he forgot the whole night, like everyone else."

Painful though it might be, it was better for both of us that Xavier recalled nothing of our dance. If he did, the Grim Reaper might prevent there from ever being a next time.

"I'm sure it'll be fine," Estelle said consolingly. "It'll be put down to the effects of the spell, right? The Grim Reaper will understand. I mean, most of the town was affected."

Even the dead. "Yeah, but he seemed confident the other night that the Grim Reaper wasn't interested in anything his apprentice got up to in his free time. Not only did it turn out not to be true, he explicitly forbade him to hang around with mortals. Meaning, me."

She winced. "I suppose he's not allowed to date humans, right?"

"The Grim Reaper never actually said that," I said. "He

just got mad at Xavier for going to a party when he was supposed to be collecting souls. I hope that as long as he only focuses on that part..."

Then what? Did I truly believe I had a chance with Xavier? He wasn't even part of the same dimension as I was, for crying out loud. He'd led me to believe the two of us were in with a shot at making it work, but who knew, maybe we'd been deluding ourselves from the start, and it had taken a magic spell to make us realise the impossible was just that—impossible.

Estelle and I reached the hotel on the seafront, which didn't appear to have suffered any lasting damage from yesterday's romantic spats. Frederick, the wizard owner, sat in the reception area, while there was no sign of Aunt Candace lurking under the windows.

I hesitated in front of the door. "Would Frederick mind us interrogating his guests? Maybe we should mention our suspicions to Edwin first. I mean, we have actual evidence now." I carried the signed book in my bag, as undeniable proof. If Ursula wasn't connected to the curse, I'd be very surprised.

"Frederick is pretty laid-back, and he knows me," Estelle commented. "I'll just pop in and ask."

As she did so, a woman sailed out of the doors, forcing us to step aside to avoid being mowed down. Her blond hair lay in coils on top of her head in a manner not dissimilar to a python, while her green dress hugged her curvy figure. Her face, bedecked in makeup, was the sort of face you saw on the covers of magazines. She had to have used magic for youthfulness as well as makeup, because she looked more my age than Aunt Candace's. Spotting Estelle and me, she gave us a dazzling smile.

"Oh, hello," she said. "I see red hair, black cloaks, and a striking family resemblance. You must be one of Candace's nieces. *Two* of you. If you were looking for your aunt, she just left."

"She did?" I said. "I mean, are you Ursula Hancock?"

"She told you all about me?" she said. "But of course she did—she and I used to be quite good friends before she went and got famous. I suppose you know all about it. I'd like to ask you a few questions, since you're here."

Argh. I thought we were the ones who were supposed to be questioning her.

"Why?" I asked. "What did you want to talk to us about? Aunt Candace?"

"Oh, my, certainly not," she said, adjusting her grip on her handbag. A scratching noise inside drew my attention. I'd heard the same noise around Aunt Candace a hundred times.

"Are you taking notes?"

She offered us another smile, this one more false-looking than the first. "I'm a reporter, and I'm here to run a story on your quaint little town. I hoped you might speak with me."

Estelle and I exchanged glances. It might be easier to bring the subject around to Aunt Candace and the curse if Ursula thought she was in control of the situation. But if she wasn't spying on her, then where had Aunt Candace gone?

"Uh, sure," I said. "Where?"

"The beach will do. There aren't many magical towns on the coast. I take it you don't have broom flight contests or anything like that?" She swept off, forcing us to run to catch up with her. Once we reached the seafront, she angled her path towards the benches overlooking the beach, which people used for picnicking in better weather.

"You're the spitting image of Candace," she told me, sitting on a bench and patting the seat next to her. As we joined her, she turned to Estelle. "You, girl, you look more like your mother. A waste of talent, I'd say, sitting on this dreary coast when that library of yours could bring in a fortune."

"Excuse me?" Estelle said. "We don't want to bring in a fortune."

"Did I imply otherwise?" Her tone was polite, but there was something beneath it as cold as the breeze sweeping off the coast.

Burying my hands in my pockets for warmth, I cleared my throat. "We actually wanted to talk to you, too," I said. "About our aunt."

"What's she done now?" she said. "She was always a troublemaker, even when we were students. A real busybody—and on a journalism course, that's saying a lot."

"She's a successful novelist now," I said, feeling compelled to defend my aunt in front of this unfriendly stranger.

"I suppose she doesn't have a choice, given… this." She indicated the waves lapping at the beach. "Why not bring in a few weather witches to make the place more appealing?"

Weather witches? I'd never heard the name, though I supposed if we could be from a family of biblio-witches, it made sense that there'd be witches with control over the weather, too.

"We don't run the town," Estelle said. "Just the library, which is open every day, rain or shine."

"Except today?" She arched a brow. "And yesterday, from what I saw."

"We held a party last night," Estelle said, not missing a beat. "To celebrate the holidays. Otherwise, the library is the main reason people visit the town. Is that what you're supposed to be writing about in your article, tourism?"

"It is," she confirmed. "I'm on a tour of magical villages and towns in the northeast of England, and I have to say, this particular corner leaves much to be desired."

"Why not come in summer?" I said. "Even Blackpool is closed and freezing at this time of year."

She gave another cold smile. "I wanted the authentic experience. I wonder if I could trouble you for a quick tour of the library?"

Ack. As long as the anti-gravity effects remained in place, there was zero chance of us opening for business. Especially if there might be space aliens on the loose.

"Perhaps another time," said Estelle. "We've decided to close early for Christmas."

"Pity," she said.

I'd had about enough of her false concern. Pulling the copy of *The Adventures of Werewolves in Cyberland* out of my pocket, I held it out to her. "Recognise this? It's addressed to you, signed by the author."

She gave a delicate laugh. "Why, yes. This is a first edition, isn't it? Your aunt sent me a copy not long after publication with a rather rude note. Naturally, I posted it back to her."

With a curse on it? I was tempted to just say it straight out, but Estelle got there first. "When was this? Recently?"

"Oh no, years ago. Before she moved back into the library, even. I suppose she must have kept it for sentimental reasons."

She has to be lying. Ursula seemed the type of person who lied for a living, which made it impossible to know if there was any truth in her words whatsoever.

"Does that seem like something she'd do?" I asked. "She's not the sentimental sort."

"I suppose not," she said, with a touch of indifference. "I know Candace, though, she can never be bothered to throw anything away. Given the state of that library, it's unsurprising. How can you stand to live in a place like that?"

Estelle shifted in her seat. "Did you just come here to get dirt on the library? Because you won't get any from us. The library is our home, and everyone from town will agree that it's the centre of Ivory Beach."

"Exactly," I added, bolstered by her unhesitant statement that the library was as much my home as it was hers.

"Really." Ursula's tone became even colder, if possible. "I heard it violates the laws of magic by its very existence. But I suppose if this is the only part of the magical world you've experienced, you can be forgiven for your ignorance."

I was starting to see why my aunt hated her so much.

"If you're looking for an argument, you won't get one from me," said Estelle, with more dislike than I'd ever heard her express. "I'd rather live here than anywhere else in the magical world."

"And you?" Ursula addressed me. "Aurora… you have even less experience of the magical world than your cousins do, as you grew up in the normal world. Are you the lost cousin she dedicated her book to?"

"You know about that?" I tried to read her expression. "So, the werewolf book isn't the only one you've read?"

"I never said I read it," she said. "I have better things to do with my time. Have you anything else you want to say about the library?"

"Only that it's our home," said Estelle. "And we wouldn't change a thing about it."

Ursula turned to me. "You must have found the place chaotic and confusing at first, if not outright dangerous."

"Actually, it's the best place I've ever been to," I said. "You can quote me on that."

"I will." She stood, her elegantly arranged hair not moving an inch in the breeze coming off the sea. "It's been nice chatting with you, children. Good day."

"Children?" I said, when she was out of earshot.

Estelle pulled a face. "In her mind, I'm still a little kid."

"You've met before?"

"When I was about five." She got to her feet. "Mum took me to visit Aunt Candace when she was at university. I don't remember much of it. What a nosy busybody. I can't believe Aunt Candace was right."

"And do you think she cursed our family?" I asked. "If she returned the book years ago, then it can't have been her."

"That doesn't let her off the hook," Estelle said. "Maybe she placed the book in the library to throw us off the trace. Either way, I don't like her. If she didn't cause the curse, it can't be a coincidence that she showed up here wanting us to badmouth the library right at the same time as the curse broke out."

"I don't disagree." I returned the signed book to my pocket. "Then we should follow her. Or chase down Aunt Candace, wherever she is, and ask her more about their history."

We retraced our steps back to the square. There, I spotted Ursula's blond head disappearing into a side street. "Where's she going?"

"That's the tourism office." Estelle stood on tip-toe, but we were too far away to see more of Ursula than her blond hair, let alone overhear her. "We need to make sure she's not telling any lies about the library. I'm sure she planned on embellishing every word we said."

"I thought so." I shuddered. "She's awful."

And just what had she made of yesterday's shenanigans? If she *had* been at the library last night, the idea of her running a story about a party in which all the guests had fainted was as unappealing as running into a space alien. Not to mention the Grim Reaper showing up. I could only imagine what she'd say to *that.*

"Rory." Estelle caught my arm. "She knows Aunt Candace has been following her. We're better off using a spell."

"An eavesdropping spell?" I took out my notebook and pen, and she did likewise.

"Not quite," she said. "Those are tricky to work with biblio-witch magic. But I can teach you an unobtrusive spell. Just write the word *hide* and focus on yourself. It won't be as strong outside the library, but it should be enough for us to stay hidden."

"Like an invisibility spell?" *Awesome.* I'd assumed that sort of spell was too advanced for my basic classes.

"Not quite," she said. "It's more that people just… overlook us, when we use that spell. We're not invisible, but we're unobtrusive. It'll work."

"Sounds good to me." I pressed the tip of my pen to the page. Then at the same time, we both wrote *hide.*

I turned to Estelle. "Can you see me?"

"Yes, but only because I already knew you were there. Nobody else will. We'd better move."

Hoping the spell was in full effect, I hurried after her. Ursula had already disappeared into a squat brick building bearing a sign proclaiming it to be Ivory Beach's tourist information office. The town did look a little drab at this time of year, with the exception of the library, but how many people in Britain took beach holidays in December? Even in summer, there was a good chance of rain. She was just trying to get a good story. Which ought to be proof enough she was responsible for the curse.

We approached the tourism office, and Estelle nudged the door open. I stepped inside and collided with something solid. Something human-shaped, invisible, crouching in the shadows…

Something shaped like Aunt Candace.

I gasped, and her hand clamped over my mouth. She must have heard Ursula mention coming here during one of her eavesdropping attempts and decided to overtake her.

Luckily for all of us, the woman sitting behind the counter was absorbed in reading a magazine and didn't look up as Estelle quietly closed the door behind us. The Aunt Candace-shaped shadow moved towards a pair of oak doors at the back of the reception area, halting outside.

Ursula's voice drifted through. "I'm very excited to

interview you about the town. I'm sure it will raise your profile in the eyes of the magical community."

"Yeah right," I said under my breath, and Aunt Candace elbowed me in the spine.

"I'm glad you're here," said another female voice. "I've heard a lot about your work. None of it favourable, I confess."

"I simply wish to paint an honest picture of the town and its various features," she said. "For instance, I heard that most people who visit this town come to the library, don't they? It seems a pity not to take advantage of that. Make it more of a public space rather than the possession of an eccentric family."

She can't be serious. My hands curled into fists at my sides.

"The Hawthorn family?" asked the other woman. "They have owned the library since its inception. The town wouldn't be the same without them."

I felt a rush of gratitude towards the stranger. Aunt Candace, meanwhile, muttered, "Obviously."

"I didn't mean to imply they aren't doing their jobs," said Ursula, in tones suggesting that was exactly what she'd implied. "I meant that if you turned it more commercial, I imagine it would draw more visitors. Does anyone even know where it came from or how it works? How do they fund all those books? I've heard some alarming stories, too, about missing corridors and rooms containing dangerous animals."

The voices dropped to murmurs, and unease skittered down my spine. Nobody in their right mind would consider changing the library, would they? More to the point, who had been telling tales about us behind our backs?

Now my suspicions were out in full force. Setting off a curse that caused havoc was a very good way to remove Aunt Adelaide's authority and make the library look even less safe than it already was. Now I understood why Aunt Candace had hidden outside. If she'd directly confronted Ursula, she'd have denied everything.

There came the sound of footsteps behind us. Uh-oh. The receptionist was on her way to the doors, and if she found the three of us hiding in the shadows, our cover would be blown. I darted to the side, tip-toeing across the reception area and taking great care not to walk into any of the others. Aunt Candace nudged the door open and we escaped into the street.

None of us spoke until we were a safe enough distance away to undo our *hide* spells. Then, I turned on Aunt Candace. "You knew?"

"I suspected," she said. "She's had her eye on the library ever since she found out it existed, and she always envied me for it. All this talk about improving the town's value to tourists is plain nonsense. She's jealous, that's all."

"Maybe she's right that the town could use more tourism in winter," said Estelle. "But that's not the point, is it? She wants a good story, and she's willing to sacrifice our livelihoods to get it. Our mum will have a fit when I tell her."

"You're going to tell her?" said Aunt Candace. "I wouldn't. She'll do something rash."

"Haven't you been implying Ursula is up to no good the whole time she's been in town?" I pulled the book out of my pocket. "This is signed and addressed to her, and it's the first book that came to life under the curse. She denied everything and claimed she returned it to you years ago. Is it true?"

"She did?" Her brow furrowed. "Perhaps. I can't recall."

Estelle groaned. "That won't be good enough for Edwin. He's occupied with that thief, besides. Just what have you been doing, following Ursula around all day?"

"Certainly not," she said. "I saw it as my mission to talk to everyone she's interviewed and ensure that none of them have damaged the library's reputation."

Wait... she was?

"Don't look so shocked," Aunt Candace added. "The library is as much my home as it is yours."

I pocketed the book again. "Did you know gravity switched off in the library today? I think it's imitating one of your sci-fi books now."

"Oh," said Aunt Candace. "That's inconvenient."'

"You're telling me," said Estelle. "The curse is still in effect, and as long as it can only be removed by the caster, we'll have to keep the place closed to everyone—especially her. I wouldn't put it past her to try and trick us into admitting what's going on, though."

"Like you tricked everyone into drinking that champagne yesterday?" Aunt Candace grinned. "Devious, aren't you?

Estelle strode towards the library. "I just want everything to go back to normal, and preferably a Christmas without curses and nosy reporters."

"Likewise. It's none of her business what's in the library." I didn't want to lose my new home. Thinking about being tossed back into the normal world made me feel cold inside

"No, but she's crafty," said Aunt Candace. "It took me this long to find out what she was reporting—" She broke off as Estelle flew into the air upon stepping over the library's threshold. "Oh, so it *is* the spaceship from my science fiction series. Excellent."

"This is not excellent," I said through gritted teeth. My own feet left the ground the instant I walked in, and I trod down hard to keep from being swept up to the ceiling. Aunt Candace bounded into the library behind us, whooping as her feet left the ground.

"I always thought this was one of my more ingenious ideas." She spun on the spot, bowing to an imaginary audience.

"You're not helping at all," I said. "Wait—what's that noise?"

There came a howling sound from above. Then a pair of shadowy tentacled shapes appeared among the bookshelves.

Those must be the space aliens.

9

The aliens were foul-looking creatures, with suction cups on their tentacles like octopi. Each had a long antenna sticking out of what I assumed was its forehead, though without any visible eyes or mouth, it was anyone's guess. *Ugh.* One thing could be said for Aunt Candace—she didn't lack for imagination.

Estelle whipped out her Biblio-Witch Inventory and tapped a word. The aliens flew into the air, but thanks to the lack of gravity, they remained floating there above our heads, tentacles flailing around. *Ugh, ugh, ugh.*

I backed up against the door—or tried to. "Aunt Candace, please tell me you know how to get rid of these things."

"Be reasonable, Rory," she said. "It's been a long time since I wrote the book."

"I remember why I gave up on that series," said Estelle. "Those sucker-headed aliens gave me nightmares."

"Now isn't the time for criticism!" Aunt Candace pulled out her pen and notebook. "Let's see..."

"Are you going to write them out of existence?" I asked.

"Oh, no, I'm making notes for a new book."

Estelle groaned. "At this rate, the only thing you'll need to write is your obituary."

"Aunt Candace, you created them." I floated out of range of the aliens' flailing tentacles. "If anyone can get rid of them, you can. Just erase them from the text. The same way I changed those invitations yesterday."

"That won't work," she said. "The books are already in print, and the curse has taken on a life of its own now. You can't burn every copy of my books in the whole world."

The aliens descended again. Estelle raised a book and hit one of them over the head, sending it spinning into its neighbour. I pulled out my Biblio-Witch Inventory, but except for the word 'rise'—which wouldn't be effective without any gravity—none of the spells I'd learned so far would be able to overcome a tentacled alien.

"Are they what the werewolves turned into?" I hit the word *rise,* but the alien floated sideways instead of up in the air. "Can't we lock them somewhere until midnight?"

"We'll have to," said Estelle. "Aunt Candace—"

"I remembered how to shut them down!" Aunt Candace said. "Twist the antenna!"

She lunged, grabbing one of the aliens by its slimy tentacle. Estelle and I exclaimed in alarm, but she gave it another thwack with the book and caught hold of the antenna on top of what must be its head. To Aunt Candace's surprise as much as ours, the alien's tentacles retracted and it flipped upside-down, looking oddly beetle-like without its tentacles.

The second alien moved in our direction. Recovering, Estelle hit it with the book, and I grabbed its antenna. One twist, and the tentacles disappeared.

"Nice going, Rory," said Estelle.

"You know," said Aunt Candace, "I think you might have made the right call in closing the library today."

"You think?" I looked up at the ceiling. "We'd better make sure no others are lurking in here."

It took us the better part of the morning to rid the library of its alien invaders, and even longer to round them up and shove them through a door into an empty classroom. We ran—or rather, floated—into Aunt Adelaide on the second floor, where a number of the closed doors had opened, their contents trying to escape into the library. After stopping to pass on the instructions about how to shut down the tentacled aliens, we resumed our quest and left Aunt Adelaide re-shelving restless books.

By the time Estelle and I reached the ground floor again, we were both panting and covered in slime from the aliens' tentacles.

"I need a shower," I said. "But I don't want to find out the hard way whether the water floats, too."

"Best not risk it." Estelle pulled out her wand and gave it a wave, and the slime vanished from our cloaks.

"Thanks," I said. "You'll have to teach me that one, assuming I ever get my hands on a wand."

A frantic cawing noise came from somewhere behind the desk. "Oh, no. I think Jet might have got stuck somewhere."

I floated towards the shelves—and right into Xavier.

The momentum sent us both sprawling into a hovering shelf, scattering books through the air.

"Oh—sorry!" I said. "I didn't know you were in here."

"I caught your familiar." He held out a hand, the little crow balanced on his fingers. "What's going on in here?"

"Someone switched off gravity," I said. "Also, fair warning, there are tentacled alien beasts on the loose. You have to twist their antenna to shut them down."

"Ah," he said, as though tentacled aliens were par for the course. "Another of your aunt's books, I'm guessing?"

"You've got it." I held out my hand and Jet hopped onto my palm, chirping.

"He saved me, partner!" he squeaked.

"Can you fly?" I asked. "You should probably hide somewhere safe in case there are any more aliens lurking around."

"Never a dull moment, is there?" remarked Xavier.

Jet chirped and bounded off my hand, half-flying, half-floating. Trusting him to find his own way to safety, I turned back to Xavier. This was the first time we'd been alone together since the party, and a not-insignificant part of me had thought he'd never want to see me again after I'd taken advantage of his spell-addled state. Or his boss would have forbidden us from seeing one another. It was hard to think of the Grim Reaper's shadowy presence when faced with Xavier's startlingly bright eyes—and the scent I hadn't noticed before last night, cool as the fresh mountain air.

Another alien floated past, replacing the cool smell with a foul stench that made me cough. "Ah—just grab the antenna. Not the tentacles."

"Like this?" He took the alien's antenna in one hand

and twisted it. *Wow, he's fast.* "Where are you putting them?"

"In a spare classroom," I said. "To make sure none of them get outside. I don't think people will be as casual about tentacled aliens as they were about knights on horseback throwing roses at people."

"You may be right." He gave the alien a push down to ground level, and between us, we steered it in the direction of the classroom. I'd never thought of our silences as awkward before, but after last night, I hadn't the faintest idea where we stood. Not on a dance floor, that was for sure.

Say something, Rory. Why did words always fail me when I needed them most?

"Your boss isn't still mad at you, is he?" I asked.

"No," he said. "Why would you think that?"

"Because you came to the party when you should have been collecting souls."

"I did?"

Oh, no. Did he not remember at all? "Last night. You were… I guess you were under the effects of the spell." So much that one drop of dosed champagne had erased the whole night.

I should be glad of it. Given the Grim Reaper's reaction, it would have been a lot worse if we'd both been in control of our actions and decisions. My own choices had been bad enough for both of us. It didn't help that he looked more gorgeous than ever today, unless it was just my knowledge that I couldn't have him that made him look more appealing.

Of course he wasn't in control of his decisions. That would have been far too good to be true.

"What are you two doing?" Cass interrupted. "It might have escaped your attention, but we're being invaded by aliens as we speak, so stop canoodling and get on with it."

"We are." I indicated the closed classroom door ahead. "We're just returning this guy to his resting place."

"And there's a dozen more on the third floor. I could use a hand."

"All right, keep your hair on." I suspected she'd interrupted on purpose, and it was far from easy to hold a serious conversation while attempting to herd unconscious aliens through a maze of floating books and down three flights of stairs. Cass remained on the third floor, disarming each tentacled creature, while Xavier and I directed them downstairs towards the classroom on the ground floor.

Partway through, Aunt Adelaide floated past, an aggrieved expression on her face. "What a waste of time… oh, it's you, Reaper."

"I thought I'd come and lend a hand." He twisted the antenna of another alien before it made a lunge for me. I caught its tail-like appendage and gave it a shove in the direction of the classroom door. The two of us floated down, Xavier holding the door open while I kicked the alien through, careful not to let any of the others drift out.

"At this rate, we'll need another classroom," I said. "I suppose I should be glad they're not poisonous at least. How did you manage to get no slime on you?"

"I'm pure and angelic?" Xavier turned around in a movement that was as graceful as one of his moves on the dance floor.

I laughed. "We look like ballet dancers."

He gave another twirl, and I laughed outright. He was

as graceful as ever, just like when he'd danced with me last night. Otherworldly, almost. And he'd picked *me* to spend time with today, even though he must suspect something had happened. Even if we could never have a relationship, that alone was enough, right?

If only some small, traitorous part of me didn't wish for the impossible.

Smiling, Xavier caught my hand, tugging me after him in the air, and I spun in dizzy circles. Laughing, I steadied myself against a bookcase. "I'm glad we kept the place closed. Imagine the academy students trying to work in here when it's like this."

"This isn't a study-friendly environment." He yanked the classroom door closed before one of the aliens could float out. "Believe it or not, this isn't the weirdest day I've had here in the library."

"I believe you," I said. "It's in my top five, though. It was worse having to run around yesterday, trying to find a way to sabotage a wedding before my aunt could make a big mistake."

"She tried to marry her ex-husband," he said. "Or am I not remembering right?"

"No… you got that right." Caution warred with the impulse to ask him to search his memories further. *Let it go, Rory. You saw the Reaper's reaction last night.* Never mind that at the time, I hadn't cared. "As soon as we're done with these aliens, I'm going to read Aunt Candace's entire backlist so I'm not unprepared for the next catastrophe."

And no more dancing. He might not remember last night, but I did, and I couldn't be trusted not to put both of us at risk from the Reaper's wrath.

Aunt Adelaide floated into view. "That's the last of

them," she said. "Rory, Estelle said the two of you have an idea who did this and you wanted to talk to me about it."

Guilt surged. Ursula was out to destroy the reputations of both the library *and* the town as a whole and here I was, dancing with the Reaper. "I do," I said. "Xavier, you don't have to stay."

"Oh." My heart sank to hear the disappointment in his voice, but I had to put the library first. "Sure, I'll see you later."

He looked like he wanted to say more, but Aunt Adelaide's bad mood warned me it was best to get this over with.

Once he'd gone, Aunt Adelaide listened in silence as Estelle and I summarised our 'interview' with Ursula and the conversation we'd overheard at the town hall.

"The interfering busybody," she muttered. "I suppose I should have listened to Candace after all."

"Ursula shouldn't be allowed to print lies about us," Estelle said.

"It sounds more like she's angling for some creative truth-telling," she said. "I bet she's spoken to the curse-breaker, for one."

"What does she have to gain from this?" I asked. "Destroying our livelihoods?"

"Candace implied she's in line for a promotion," said Aunt Adelaide. "There might be more to it than that, but I confess I've been distracted this week."

No kidding. The timing was way too suspicious for my liking. If anyone had something to gain from throwing the library into chaos, it was Ursula.

"Still," said Estelle. "There's no reason for anyone else in the town to want to destroy our reputations, right?"

"No, but it's complicated," said Aunt Adelaide. "Some people have never liked that the power in the town landed on our heads because nobody outside of our family is able to manipulate the library. And you know how it feels about outsiders. Most assistants we've hired have quit. Granted, the library seems much easier to manage these days, particularly since your arrival, Rory."

I shifted uncomfortably. "Uh, but this spell… it's not under any of our control, right? I mean, if it gets outside the library, then we might end up blamed."

I looked around the lobby for Aunt Candace, but she'd slipped away, probably to write the alien 'attack' into a future book. The magical world didn't have quite the level of health and safety rules as the normal world, but if the police weren't occupied with the thief, then they might well have figured out we were at the centre of the chaos.

"You're not wrong," she said. "I can thank your quick thinking—and yours, too, Estelle—that the situation hasn't worsened. The Reaper will keep quiet, won't he?"

"Who—Xavier?" I said. "Of course he won't tell his boss. He doesn't remember last night, either."

I felt Estelle's questioning eyes on me, but I didn't need to be distracted now. Not with so much at stake.

"Good," she said. "Most people come into the town to see the library—everyone knows that. Her attempts to put us down might even bring *more* visitors."

"Not if they find out we're under a curse," I said. "It seems to be cycling through Aunt Candace's books, right? Doesn't she have a horror pen name?"

"I don't recall." Her brow furrowed. "As well as her sci-fi name, there's also her fantasy adventures—and the one book she wrote under her real name."

"The one about my dad's life story." My heart lurched. "Could *that* come to life?"

"The books aren't real," Aunt Adelaide said firmly. "And we'll put a stop to this. I intend to contact Ursula Hancock and see if she objects to a direct interview with the library's owner. I highly doubt she'd turn me down."

No, but she still might find a way to twist whatever you say according to her own agenda. "I hope you're right. If we proved she was the one who set the curse off, we'd be able to get her kicked out of town and the interview pulled from publication, right?"

"Of course," she said. "I will call and see what she has to say. If Ursula did set the curse off, only she can reverse it, so keep that book somewhere safe, Rory."

"I will." I'd stashed the book in my bag along with my dad's journal, just in case.

Estelle shook her head as Aunt Adelaide floated towards the family's living quarters, presumably to call Ursula and arrange an interview. "I'm not sure this will work. She's determined to get a story out of us, and as long as the curse is active, playing along with her will only make things worse."

"I know," I said. "Perhaps your mum's intending to trick her into confessing?"

"That woman can spin a lie out of a needle and thread," Estelle said. I'd never seen her dislike someone quite that much—the curse-breaker included.

"If anyone *has* been gossiping about us behind our backs, she doesn't need to," I said. "You don't think the curse-breaker might have given her any ammunition, do you?"

She looked at the door, then at me. "I hope not. I'll go

and speak to him. Rory—your familiar hasn't spoken to her, has he?"

"I hope not." Slightly worried, I floated across the lobby, hoping Jet had taken my advice and got out of the aliens' reach. Before I reached it, though, the door opened.

The leader of the vampires entered the library and gave me a smile.

10

Every muscle in my body locked into place, remembering how it felt to be grabbed and held hostage by a vampire. If Evangeline had been allowed past the defences, she couldn't mean me any harm, but even floating in mid-air, the vampires' leader exuded a sense of menace. She wore a long black dress with an elegant collar exposing her moon-pale skin. Her dark eyes glittered, and her hair tumbled past her shoulders like a waterfall. She looked as though she'd just stepped off a stage, but the calculating glint in her eye marked her as the predator she really was.

"Don't worry, Aurora," she said. "I have no intention of harming you."

Uh-huh. I fixed my attention on a crack in the front desk, hoping she hadn't picked up on any of my stray thoughts. I'd been afraid of vampires ever since my first induction into the magical world, but that fear had increased tenfold when my aunt's ex, Dominic, had given me a letter before his untimely death, telling me not to show Evangeline my dad's old journal.

A society of vampires who hunted for lost artefacts had nearly killed me over that same journal... which happened to be in my bag.

This was the first time Evangeline had stepped foot in the library since she'd expressed an interested in looking at the journal, and what with the chaos of the last week, all my half-conceived plans to distract her had flown out of my head. Aside from the obvious.

"We're not open today," I said. "We're having difficulties with some of our books."

I'd let her work out if I meant the ones floating off the shelves, or the ones coming to life and leaving a trail of havoc behind them. For all I knew, vampires were terrified of aliens with tentacles, but I'd prefer not to give her any more ammunition against my family. Whatever she wanted the journal for, she was no friend of ours.

"I do not intend to intrude on your thoughts today, Aurora," she said. "As a matter of fact, I wanted to offer you my help."

I blinked. "With what?"

"With the curse, of course," she said. "I went to visit Edwin today, to discuss the disturbing matter of the thief hiding in our town."

"Edwin asked for your help?" Odd. She'd been downright dismissive of the police when she'd been targeted by thieves herself—granted, they'd been teenage mortals reckless enough to risk their lives stealing from the vampires. Still, I didn't believe for a minute the leader of the local vampires would offer us anything for free. She was too old, too clever, and too calculating by half.

"Yes," she said. "I turned down Edwin's request to help him find the thief. We have taken significant measures to protect our territory, so the Magpie is unlikely to try his luck there." She gave a smile that implied any thief who stepped within a mile of the vampires would live to regret it. Vampires—always looking out for their own, and for nobody else.

"So Edwin told you about the curse?" He'd been so preoccupied with the thief when we'd visited that I'd assumed he'd dismissed the curse as a harmless prank.

"Why, Aurora, one might assume you had mind-reading powers of your own," she said. "Yes, he mentioned you appeared to be afflicted by a curse… a Manifestation Curse, if I'm guessing correctly. I haven't seen one of those in a while."

"You've seen one?" *Idiot, Rory. She's over a thousand years old. She's probably seen it all.*

She smiled. "Yes, I have. It can be a very unpleasant curse in the wrong hands. When the imaginary becomes real, even temporarily, the consequences can be tragic."

"I have no idea what you're talking about." A chill raced down my back. *She's trying to manipulate me into asking her for help, so she can ask for the journal in exchange.* "I thought you came to offer me help. Not to… warn me, or whatever it is you're doing." Other than creeping me out, that is.

"I did," she said. "I merely wanted to give you a warning not to believe everything you see and hear. The Manifestation Curse… I can think of only one occasion in which it turned out to be permanent, and we're standing in it right now."

My jaw dropped. "The library."

She gave another smile. "Correct. This library is living proof of the power of imagination. Doubtless this is a rare and dangerous curse, but I can offer you information..."

For a price. Right?

Sure enough, she said, "In exchange for your father's journal. I understand it holds some sentimental value for you, but you must know you have no real use for an old book nobody can read. I'd be willing to pay you handsomely for it."

"No, thanks," I said, the merest tremor in my voice. "I think we can handle this ourselves. We already have our suspect under watch, and we plan on reversing the curse once we get a confession."

I hope. Even if we had it wrong and Ursula was innocent, nothing was worth sacrificing my father's journal for. Especially when Dominic had died with a warning in his hand telling me never to let Evangeline see it.

"I thought you'd say that," Evangeline said. "Good day."

And she was gone in the blink of an eye, leaving nothing behind but the merest impression on my eyelids.

I released a steadying breath, and a clattering noise came from behind the shelves. A moment later, Cass floated into view, her arms crossed over her chest. "What the bloody hell are you doing making bargains with the vampires?"

"She didn't exactly leave me much choice," I said. "Besides, I refused to accept her trade."

"You don't *refuse* the leader of the vampires." Her eyes narrowed. "First the Reaper and now her. Are you *trying* to get us blacklisted?"

"She already hates us," I pointed out. "Also, Ursula set off the curse, so it's a waste of time us making a deal with the vampires for the same information. She wouldn't know about it if she hadn't swiped the information from Edwin's mind in the first place."

Cass's lips pursed. "No, but the vampires make their own rules. She'll get you back for it later."

"You'd be mad at me for making a deal with the vampires' leader without asking permission, anyway, so there's no winning here," I pointed out. "Also, Edwin tried to make a deal with her, too, to get her to help him find that thief. She said no. It's not worth making deals with her when she's looking out for her own people and nobody else."

"Am I supposed to care?" She floated past, wrinkling her nose. "Those aliens smell like a drain. Also, I heard your familiar crying from inside your room, so he might be stuck somewhere."

"Ah, no." If the main part of the library was anything to go by, my possessions were probably scattered all over the place.

I floated into the corridor to our living quarters and upstairs, bumping into the walls several times on the way up. Bruised and irritable, I opened my bedroom door to find every one of my possessions hovering on the ceiling. Jet let out a wailing noise from behind a bookshelf, and I let him out. He floated past, grabbing a book with his clawed feet for balance.

I pulled down a couple of books and tried to return them to the shelf, then gave up. I hadn't a hope of fixing the place without gravity functioning. I turned around and saw Jet floating in the middle of the room, clinging onto a photo album.

"I forgot I even had this." I caught hold of the album

and tugged it into my hands. It was one of the few photo albums I had, since Dad had kept few photos of his family around the house. Now I knew why: because he'd had to keep the magical world a secret. But there were plenty of photos of the two of us, and Mum, before her death. I flipped open the album, my chest tightening as I took in the images of our little family. Sitting on the beach, having picnics in the park, playing in the garden of the old house. The most recent picture was one Aunt Adelaide had given to me: a photograph of Dad, Aunt Adelaide, Aunt Candace and Grandma, taken before I was even born. Dad looked so happy. They all did. This was a rare snapshot of his old life, before he'd met Mum and left the library. I could see the shape of the library's balconies and shelves behind his head, indicating the photo had been taken in the middle of the ground floor. We'd stood in the same spot a hundred times, yet we'd never stand there at the same time.

I closed the album, my eyes stinging. It was no use dwelling on the past, and yet as long as the curse remained active, the library's future was out of our hands.

I woke up what felt like ten seconds after I'd fallen asleep when a huge crash resonated through the library. My bed hit the floor hard, and more thumps and thuds sounded when my bookcase fell to the floor, along with its contents. I shielded my head from falling books with my arms, and the covers landed on top of me in a tangle.

That'll be gravity turning back on.

I lay there for a moment, wondering if I should try to

clean up the mess now or if it would be better to wait until morning.

As it turned out, though, I didn't need to. Magic rippled through the room, and everything returned to its place. Books slid back onto shelves, while the covers tucked themselves into the bed without me moving an inch. Either the library's magic had cleaned up the mess, or Aunt Adelaide was awake. She'd retired to bed early and hadn't spoken to us much last night. We'd all taken our meals separately rather than eating together as a family, so I hadn't had the chance to talk to her about Evangeline's offer.

I got out of bed, threw on a dressing gown, and walked downstairs. There, Aunt Adelaide sat alone in the living room, meditatively sipping a cup of herbal tea.

"Can't sleep?" she asked.

"Gravity hit me hard." I gestured around at the shelves, which were the same as ever, including the stacks of Aunt Candace's books on the table. "Did you put it all back or did the library's magic do it?"

"Both," she said. "Want to join me? There's plenty for both of us." She conjured up a second mug from the kitchen, filling it with a wave of her wand.

"Oh, thanks," I said, accepting the mug. "I guess the others will have woken up, too."

"Not necessarily. Candace can sleep through an earthquake. And if Cass was awake, we'd have heard her yelling."

"Sounds about right." I smiled. "There's something I wanted to talk to you about."

I recounted Evangeline's surprising visit and her offer, as well as my response.

"Was I wrong to turn her down?" I asked. "I know she was trying to manipulate me, and we're almost certain Ursula did it—but if she didn't, then Evangeline might have been able to help us."

"It wouldn't be worth the risk," said Aunt Adelaide. "I don't know what she wants with that journal, but it can't be anything good."

I thought back to my first introduction to the paranormal world, when Mortimer Vale and his two companions had crashed into my life. "Might she be involved with... them?"

"I doubt it. Most likely, she wants it for her private collection."

"She mentioned having new security measures in place since those kids tried to rob her," I added. "She read the information on the curse from Edwin's mind. If it turns out our guess is wrong, she might use it against us."

"I doubt she will," said Aunt Adelaide. "She rarely concerns herself with matters which she deems trivial. Besides, it wouldn't be in her interests to cause damage to our livelihoods."

"I hope you're right," I said. "She also said she'd encountered a Manifestation Curse once before. And... and she implied a similar curse created the library."

There was a long pause, in which Aunt Adelaide took a sip of her drink. "She's incorrect. A curse may have created some of the library's more... eccentric features, but it used to be our family's home long before my mother transformed it. If the curse were undone, we'd still be here."

"So—she was just guessing?" That didn't seem right, but even a mind-reader like Evangeline didn't know everything. Even Sylvester and the question room didn't. Now I thought about it, I hadn't seen him all day. Given the lack of gravity, it wasn't surprising he'd hidden somewhere until the storm blew over. "When did it happen?"

"The library? It was a gradual transformation," she said. "My mother worked on it a section at a time... there was a phase when new corridors would appear overnight. After our mother's death, your aunt and I inherited the library and all that comes along with it, and for the most part, the town's citizens are grateful."

"So you don't think Ursula will find many people to badmouth us behind our backs?" I asked.

"No," she said. "Most likely, she'll embellish the truth and try to weave a story from every detail she can glean."

"But you're still doing the interview with her tomorrow?"

She dipped her head. "Yes. I intend to find out just what type of magic she's working. Few have the skill to pull off a Manifestation Curse, so if it *is* her, she must have had help."

Hmm. "So will it keep cycling through different books each day? Mr Bennet hinted it might last for months, unless the person who set it off is able to reverse it. But Ursula denied ever having owned the book..."

"She said the same when I called her," said Aunt Adelaide. "I'm sure she'll change her mind when I speak with her face to face. She's certainly an accomplished liar, if one with an obvious agenda. I suppose I should be grateful that she didn't have a wedding to report on. I never did thank you properly, Rory, for stopping me from going ahead with it. I knew I made the right choice in inviting you to live here in the library."

My face heated with a pleased flush. "Um, Aunt Adelaide, I have a weird question. Do you have any more photos of my dad? He never had any at home."

"Of course." She stood, moving around the living room and reaching for a picture frame on the mantlepiece. "We had this one printed several times."

I took the picture from her. It had been taken in the Reading Corner, judging by the pattern of the shelves in the background. Dad and Aunt Candace stood side by side, with Aunt Adelaide—obviously pregnant—and Grandma on the other side.

"That was shortly before Estelle was born," said Aunt Adelaide.

"She's a few months older than me," I said. "So does that mean...?"

"Your parents were already married? Of course. That was your father's last visit to the library before your birth."

I looked intently at the picture, as though if I stared hard enough, Dad would look right back at me and tell me everything would be okay. Blinking hard, I handed the photograph back to Aunt Adelaide and scanned the pile of books on the table. The copy of *Entranced by the Normal* on top was battered-looking, as though someone had thumbed through it a number of times. I opened the cover, reading the dedication. *To the lost cousin.*

I turned the pages, pausing as a photograph fell out. I picked it up, my heart swooping. In the picture, Dad and Mum stood close to the camera, his arm around her shoulder. "Hey... this is one of their wedding photos. I've seen this one."

I had a copy somewhere upstairs. Aunt Candace and

Aunt Adelaide weren't to be seen, which came as no surprise—like at the funeral, they'd have been forced to keep their distance to avoid being spotted by the normals.

"Oh, we were there," said Aunt Adelaide. She scrutinised the photo and pointed to the back. "You can see us in the background if you look closely."

"I can?" I scanned the rows of unfamiliar faces. "Mum picked the bridesmaids. I guess I know why now. I don't know who the best man is…"

"A friend of your dad's," she said. "A normal."

"I'd have thought it would have been Abe." I spotted the man himself standing separate from the crowd, wearing his usual sullen expression even surrounded by happy faces. I was sure the best man looked familiar, but then again, everyone did. I *had* met them before, in my old life.

As for my new life? The library seemed a thousand times more real to me than the past. It was my home, and like my dad, I'd do everything I could to protect it.

Dawn came with an alarming neighing noise that cut through my dreams and jolted me from sleep almost as effectively as gravity turning back on. Instantly alert, I rolled out of bed and opened my bedroom door to find Estelle standing in the corridor. "What is that?"

"I was about to find out." She was fully dressed, her sleeves rolled up and her wand in her hand. "Sounds like a horse."

I groaned. "Not again. Is it another replay of the romance novels?"

"Considering a troll just went rampaging past downstairs, I hope not."

"Troll?" I winced at the sound of another loud neigh. Reaching the stairs, I peered down to see a horse standing at the bottom of the staircase. "I think he might need a hand."

"On it." Estelle waved her wand and the horse lifted his front legs from the stairs, backing up into the corridor. "Get your Biblio-Witch Inventory, Rory—you'll need it."

I ran back into my room and closed the door before searching for my clothes and Biblio-Witch Inventory. At least I'd showered in the middle of the night after gravity had turned back on and the water was no longer in any danger of floating from the en-suite bathroom into my bedroom. Heaven knew what it might get up to today.

Once I'd thrown on my clothes and found my Biblio-Witch Inventory, I joined Estelle in coaxing the startled horse away from the stairs. For once, I was grateful for the time I'd spent helping Cass deal with her pet kelpie.

"What in the goddess's name is going on?" Aunt Adelaide poked her head out of the kitchen. "Don't tell me those knights are back."

"Nah," said Cass, striding out of the living room into the hall. "You're not acting like a lovesick teenager, for a start. Whose horse is this?"

"Whoever it belongs to, it can't stay in here," said Aunt Adelaide. "Ursula has insisted on conducting our interview in the library."

"She what?" said Estelle. "That's not her call to make."

"If I turn her down, she'll print a story full of rumours about what we're hiding in here," said Aunt Adelaide, looking disgruntled. "Gravity is working. You can keep any interferences from getting into a single interview room, can't you?"

"Uh..." I looked at Estelle. "It depends what type of disturbances they are. Are you sure about this?"

"You think being in the library will convince her to confess to using the curse on us?" said Cass, stroking the horse's mane.

"I believe I can convince her," Aunt Adelaide said. "Has anyone seen Sylvester?"

"I assumed he was hiding from the curse." Cass followed the horse into the lobby, still stroking its mane. "When are they coming?"

"In ten—" The doorbell rang. "Minutes."

"Or seconds," said Cass, grabbing the horse's reins. "I'll get him out of the way."

"Do that," said Aunt Adelaide distractedly. "Estelle, Rory, fetch Candace and Sylvester, won't you? And keep that horse somewhere out of sight."

Nobody objected. In the time it took Aunt Adelaide to reach the door, the three of us collectively managed to hide the horse in the reference section, where Cass conjured up an apple to keep it quiet.

"Where was that troll?" I whispered to Estelle.

"I locked him in a spare room. I hope they don't pick that one for the interview."

Cass swore under her breath. "This had better be worth it."

I peered through the shelves as Ursula strode into the library, wearing a vibrant yellow dress. As before, her hair coiled on top of her head and makeup adorned her face.

"Come this way." Aunt Adelaide beckoned her into the library.

Estelle leaned closer to me. "Rory, I'll go and make sure Ursula doesn't see or hear anything she's not supposed to. Can you find Aunt Candace and Sylvester?"

"Will do." I held my breath as the horse let out a whinnying noise.

"What is that?" asked Ursula.

"The Magical Creatures Division comes with its own sound effects," said Aunt Adelaide. "We'll quieten it down—Rory, do handle that, if you don't mind. This way."

As they headed through the Reading Corner towards the meeting rooms at the back, I leaned closer to Cass. "I'm going to find Aunt Candace and Sylvester. Can you take care of the horse?"

"Of course," she said, as though I was a fool for doubting her ability to take care of a new surprise pet. Knowing her, she'd have it tamed and living in the Magical Creature's Division by the day's end.

Better than everything floating. But now I thought about it, I hadn't seen Sylvester in days. It wasn't unusual for him to avoid trouble, but I couldn't recall him ever being absent for so long before.

I backed away from the horse, listening out. From the silence, they must have entered the interview room. The library was cleaner than usual—probably because we hadn't had people in here for an extended length of time since the curse had manifested—but that made the absence of the others even more obvious. It would be helpful if the library had the magical equivalent of CCTV so I could find people when they wandered off.

"Sylvester," I whispered. "Jet—hey, Jet."

An instant later, the crow landed on my hand. "How may I help you, partner?"

"Have you seen Sylvester lately?"

The crow shuffled his feathers. "No, partner."

Frowning, I returned to the front desk and searched for the book of questions, but the anti-gravity spell had reshuffled all the books that hadn't been on the shelves, and searching through all of them would take hours.

"What are you doing?" Cass hissed at me from behind the shelf. "I thought you were looking for Sylvester."

"He isn't answering."

There was a loud crashing noise from upstairs. Uh-oh.

"Go and see what that was," Cass said. "And please stop it from getting into the interview room."

"That's the plan." A 'please' from Cass was a sign of how seriously she was taking the situation—but even that might not help if Sylvester had pulled a disappearing act.

I kept Jet on my shoulder as I made for the stairs, moving in such a hurry that I tripped into one of the trick stairs. My legs kicked at thin air, and I pulled myself onto the next stair, expecting to hear Sylvester's derisive comments. No sound came except for Jet's agitated chirping. *Something's wrong.* Sylvester might be unpredictable, but he *was* the library, and he wouldn't abandon us in a crisis. What if he wasn't off doing his own thing, but missing? Or affected by the curse?

"Hey, Sylvester," I called out. "You won't believe me, but I'm starting to worry about you. Are you okay?"

Silence. I carried on climbing the stairs, though I hadn't the faintest idea where the owl spent the time he wasn't flying around annoying people and returning books to their shelves. But now I thought about it, if there was a way of undoing the curse, it must lie in the forbidden room. I should have gone in there from the start. The room might not be able to point out the culprit, but if the library itself was created using a Manifestation Curse, the answers would likely be in the room which knew almost everything. Or rather, Sylvester did, and he was conspicuously absent at the moment.

But if Sylvester and the forbidden room's book were gone and Ursula *hadn't* done it… how would we ever find the culprit?

11

The staircase to the third floor brought me to the source of the noise. Several tall figures with pointed ears had knocked over a bookcase, while Aunt Candace lurked behind the shelves, frantically scribbling in a notebook.

"Aunt Candace!" I hissed. "You're needed downstairs. Now."

"I trust my sister to do an adequate job with the interview," she said. "I'd rather not give Ursula any more excuses to badmouth me."

"And this won't?" I gestured to the people sitting on the collapsed bookcase, which they appeared to have turned into a picnic table. "Who are they?"

"Elves, of course."

"I thought elves were four feet tall, like Edwin."

"Not in my books, they aren't," she said. "I heard normals find this kind of elf more appealing."

"Aunt Candace," I said, with more patience than she deserved, "it might have escaped your attention, but there's a reporter fishing for dirt on us and interrogating your sister as we speak, Sylvester is missing, and Cass is trying to stop a horse from rampaging across the ground floor."

"It sounds like you're handling it," she said. "I've never had the opportunity to eavesdrop on my own characters before and I'm not going to miss it."

She's impossible. "Have you at least seen Sylvester?"

"No. I expect he's hiding, if he's got any sense."

I'm not sure you *do.* Teeth clenched, I left her to her eavesdropping and returned to the stairs. Voices drifted up from below. The interview was over already?

I hurried down to the ground floor and ducked behind a bookshelf to listen in.

"That was most illuminating, Adelaide, thank you," said Ursula.

"Any time," replied Aunt Adelaide. "Do contact me when the interview is printed."

"Naturally," she said. "And please, let me know if you change your mind about giving us a tour. I rather think this curse has undone the public's trust in the library. I heard there were a number of complaints in the last week from people who attended a party here and woke up with a terrible case of memory loss."

The cheek of it. She must know perfectly well what had happened. From an outsider's perspective, it wasn't hard to guess, but considering nobody else even came close to fitting the profile of the caster, it *must* be Ursula's doing. I'd hoped to come down to find the police on the doorstep, but Aunt Adelaide and Estelle had their public faces on as they showed Ursula to the door.

"The library wasn't responsible for the curse," Aunt

Adelaide said in a firm voice. "It seems to be the result of outside interference, perhaps a prank by someone with a reason to amuse themselves with our misfortune."

"Prank or not, I have to confess I'm surprised you took no action to prevent the curse from spreading to the rest of town."

"There is nothing to be done against a curse of this nature," she said. "Unless the caster decides to undo it, we must wait until it runs its course. Nobody has come to harm as a result, and it is certainly no more dangerous than anything else in the magical world."

"I suppose you know best," said Ursula, sweeping towards the doors. "I look forward to writing your story."

And she was gone, the oak doors swinging shut behind her.

"I thought she was getting arrested." I turned to face Estelle. "Did she not confess?"

"Not a word," she said. "She kept trying to turn it around, bringing up stories of times things have gone sideways in the library. I swear she's been fishing for gossip all around town. Where's Aunt Candace?"

"Eavesdropping on a pack of elves up on the third floor." Worry rose within me. "And Sylvester—I think he's missing. So you *don't* think she set off the curse, or did she slither out of answering any questions?"

"The latter," Aunt Adelaide said. Her voice was calm, which meant she was hopping mad. Dad used to sound the same on the rare occasions he lost his temper. "If I didn't know her for a witch, I'd suspect her of being a serpent shifter."

"Hey, snakes are intelligent," Cass protested. "And is

nobody going to come and help me with this horse? He's making a bloody racket over here."

"I'll help." Estelle ran over to her.

"So she didn't give anything away?" I asked Aunt Adelaide.

"I caught her trying to bug the room a couple of times, but she was subtle about it. I suspect it's why she gets so much personal information out of her interviewees."

"That's illegal, isn't it?" I said.

"Only if we proved it was her," Estelle said over her shoulder. "Every time we tried to bring up the cursed book, she insisted she returned it years ago. Then she asked to borrow copies of two more of Aunt Candace's books, so we had to pretend we'd run out. She wanted to read *Entranced by the Normal.*"

"My dad's life story," I said. "What's it to her? Why is she so interested in our family?"

"She's interested in getting a good story," said Aunt Adelaide. "And she doesn't much care how many lives she ruins in the process."

"I can't stand her," Estelle said. "And I like most people."

"But she must have set off the curse," I said. "Right?"

"She claimed she had an alibi for when the curse went off, which is true," said Aunt Adelaide. "She's never been to the library until this morning, for a start. It's unlikely that the curse remained dormant until she entered town. Unless she had help."

I blinked. "You think someone else set off the curse? Someone who was in the library at the time?"

"She has an accomplice," Estelle said. "She must do.

They wouldn't need to be skilled enough to use the curse themselves if she already set it up."

"Exactly," said Aunt Adelaide. "If we find her accomplice…"

"Then we'll get her," Estelle said. "We'll question everyone who was in the library the day the curse went off. I'll make a list."

"There's no need," said Aunt Adelaide. "I already made one, just in case." With a flick of her wand, a piece of paper appeared in her hand. Another flick, and the list duplicated itself.

"If her accomplice was in the library, maybe they set the boggart loose as a diversion." I should have guessed there was more to the situation than Cass's habit of not locking her pets' cages.

"Maybe." Estelle took a copy of the list from her mother. "We'll go and question them, right, Rory?"

"Sure."

I followed Estelle out of the library, and we paused on the doorstep to check the list.

"The first suspect is called Gareth," said Estelle. "He's a werewolf, and he lives just off the high street. We'll go there first."

He must be the shifter who was glaring at me in the pub.

The last-minute Christmas shoppers were out in full force today, causing us to have to walk around packs of bag-laden witches and wizards. The cobbled high street wound uphill, and on either side lay shops decked out in Christmas decorations, rammed with frazzled shoppers grabbing last-minute bargains. It took several minutes of dodging people before we managed to squeeze into a side street where a number of houses were divided up into apartments. As we rang the doorbell for the werewolf's flat, a young blond witch wearing a pink cloak and hat walked out the door of the apartment block.

"Oh, hi," said Estelle. "We were wondering—is Gareth in?"

"He's in jail," said the witch. "He was caught stealing from the wand shop."

"Really?" Estelle's voice rose in surprise.

"Yes," said the witch. "I suppose he was desperate after he lost his job the other week. If you'll excuse me, I have some last-minute shopping to do."

She walked past us to the high street, and Estelle and I exchanged bewildered glances. Maybe Ursula wasn't the only person in town up to no good. Unless that thief was rubbing off on people.

"What d'you reckon?" I asked. "He was in the library when the curse first started, and I saw him in the pub afterwards. He gave me a really dirty look, but I figured it was because he took those werewolves' appearance as a personal offence."

"Weird," she said. "Maybe he set the boggart loose so nobody would notice him kick-start the curse, but I'm pretty sure I've never spoken to him before. I'm not sure werewolves can set off a curse even if it's set up by someone else, either."

"Should we check into the wand shop and ask?" I turned away from the apartment block. "For all we know, this isn't his only crime. Or maybe the police are getting so desperate to catch the thief that they're arresting innocent people."

That seemed unlikely... unless his actions were yet another side effect of the curse. With the town in the grip of holiday madness, he *might* have cracked in an attempt to get a last-minute present, but after the week I'd had, my suspicions were out in full force.

"I suppose there's no harm in asking," she said.

Since the wand shop was right in the middle of the high street, we had to fight our way through the crowds to get there. As we reached the doors, the blond witch from earlier staggered out of the apothecary, struggling to support the weight of a hefty bronze cauldron. She refused Estelle's offer of help and levitated it down the street.

"I wouldn't know if any of this was out of Aunt Candace's books," I remarked, ducking into the wand shop. As before, it was staffed by a single teenage assistant, looking even more frazzled than he had the last time I've been here.

"Please tell me you're not here to test another wand," he said.

"Oh, we're not," Estelle said. "We just heard about the break-in and we wondered if the wands were okay."

"I wasn't here," he said. "But Mr Hale was."

The old wizard cleared his throat from behind a shelf. "Back so soon?"

"We aren't wand-shopping this time," I said. "We heard about the break-in. Did he take anything?"

He glanced at the box-covered shelves. "No. I installed new defences after that Magpie incident and caught the thief red-handed before he had the chance to take one further step into the shop."

"Why would a werewolf steal from a wand shop, anyway?" I asked. "I heard he lost his job, but he wouldn't have any use for magical accessories."

"He pulled out a bogus story and refused to say anything more." The old man coughed. "We'll see if some time in a prison cell loosens his tongue."

"Hmm," said Estelle. "We're looking for a criminal ourselves, but not a thief. I don't know if you heard, but someone set a curse loose in the library this week. The wolf who broke into your shop was one of the suspects."

"Interesting," he commented. "The thief already took one wand, so it may be that he had his eye on the same prize, but a wand wouldn't be much use to a werewolf. I'll keep an eye out, though. As for that curse of yours, it sounds like someone has a real grudge against your family."

Not necessarily. But now I thought about it, the thief and Ursula Hancock had arrived in town around the same time. Not that either of those things explained Gareth's sudden urge to steal a wand. As far as I knew, the werewolf had already lived here and had zero connection to either of those people.

"Thanks for speaking to us," said Estelle. "We should head out."

We left the shop, swept up into the crowd's madness once again. When the high street spat us out into the town square, I turned to the clock tower. "Maybe we should go to the jail and see what Gareth's story is."

"We're supposed to be interrogating the suspects," Estelle said. "But it *is* odd for a werewolf to burgle a wand shop. I thought he had a shady look when we talked to him in the library on the day the curse went off, to tell you the truth."

"I wonder if that's why he was glaring at me in the pub," I said. "Maybe it's too much to hope for that Edwin will be distracted enough by the Magpie to let us speak to him, but it's worth a try."

Luckily, the seafront was almost deserted compared to the high street. We had no trouble reaching the police station. The interior was full of even more pictures of the thief, while Edwin sat in the middle of a small mountain of documents.

"What's your aunt done now?" he asked.

"Nothing," I said. "Why would you think that?"

He grunted. "I've been hearing stories. That friend of hers has been sniffing about the place."

"Ursula tried to get into the jail?" Estelle said. "Please tell me you didn't let her in."

"Of course not," said Edwin. "She asked me for interviews three times, but I refused. What do you want, then?"

I blinked at his surprising bluntness. "We're looking to speak with the people who were in the library at the time the curse went off, and we were told one of them is in your jail. Gareth, a werewolf. He was caught breaking into the wand shop, right?"

"Yes, he was," he said. "His trial is set for tomorrow, but due to the holidays, everything has been delayed."

"And no more news on the thief?" I moved over to the wall display showing the Magpie's movements, listing all the places he'd stolen from and showing photographs of the various signatures he'd left behind. The thief himself was believed to be a wizard, not a werewolf, judging by the magical signatures he left at each crime scene—but why would both he and Gareth attempt to rob the same shop in the space of a week? And what about Ursula? Was her arrival in town at the same time as the thief a simple coincidence?

Edwin scowled. "No. There seems to be no pattern to his targets, either. He doesn't always take valuables. Yesterday, he stole a heap of chocolate goblins from the sweet shop."

"Maybe he's a fan of chocolate," I said.

Estelle glanced at me but didn't comment. I couldn't think why a nosy reporter might steal sweets—except in an attempt to drum up a story on our high crime rate, maybe. But why single out our town in particular, except to get at Aunt Candace? A grudge alone wasn't worth this much trouble. Besides, every piece of evidence painstakingly stapled to the wall indicated the thief was male.

Edwin looked up at me. "If you wish to question the werewolf, it'll have to wait until after his trial."

"But the curse is in effect now," said Estelle. "Gravity switched off in the library yesterday. Today, there's a pack of elves on the loose and a troll locked up downstairs. They're not even real, so they can't be jailed for bad behaviour. We need to find out who did this, or I can't promise this won't ruin everyone's holidays."

His lips pressed together. "Your aunt will owe me a favour for this. Pascal, bring in Gareth. Make sure he's handcuffed."

The troll grunted and sloped through the back door which connected the town's police office with the jail.

"Thank you," I said. "This will really help us."

"It will," said Estelle, leaning to examine the wall display. "I don't mean to intrude, but did you run a background check on Ursula Hancock before she entered the town?"

"We can hardly check the backgrounds of every single person who comes here for a holiday," he said. "She showed the hotel proof of her identity and her reporter status, and that's enough for me."

Two trolls marched in, pulling Gareth between them and dragging him into a side room. Estelle and I followed close behind, where the troll deposited the shaking werewolf into a seat. His hands were cuffed, and he looked rather frightened. "I didn't do it."

"Do what?" Estelle asked.

Gareth visibly deflated. "I didn't know the shop was covered in security wards."

"What, the wand shop?" I asked. "You must have known they'd increase security after the thief tried to break in. What were you even looking for in there?"

"Thief? No. I was planting a... a recording spell."

"To eavesdrop," Estelle said, her voice sharp. "You're with Ursula."

"Not *with* her," he mumbled. "She asked for a favour in exchange for keeping the pack out of her stories. That's all. I needed the money, okay?"

"You didn't just bug the wand shop," I said. "You bugged the library, too."

"I assumed you had nothing to hide," he mumbled.

"Not if you set the curse off," I said.

"What curse?" He blinked. "I can't use magic."

"I know you can't," Estelle said. "You mean to confess that Ursula sent you to bug the library on her orders?"

"She did," he said. "She asked me to do the same to the wand shop, but I got caught. I didn't steal anything. And she's—she's going to kill me for this. Please, take me back to my cell."

Estelle and I both blinked at him. Our instincts had been wrong. He wasn't the thief *or* the person who'd set up the curse, though he was walking proof that Ursula was willing to skirt the law to get what she wanted.

"I hope you recorded that," Estelle said to Edwin. "Ursula broke the law by sending him into the library. Where did you leave the recording spell?"

"In… in a book," he mumbled.

"That's enough." Edwin ushered us back out into the lobby. "Gareth will be taken back to his cell, and we'll decide his sentence after the trial."

"A book?" I said. "We might never find it."

"You aren't wrong," said Estelle. "Thanks to the anti-gravity spell, it might be anywhere. But I guess Ursula didn't curse us after all."

"I guess not." Dissatisfied, I looked at the photographs on the wall beside Edwin's desk. The thief wore a hood in most of them, but something about the cast of his features appeared vaguely familiar to me. Not familiar enough to place, though.

"We should go," said Estelle. "My mum will want to know why we haven't talked to the other suspects yet."

"We have to tell her about this," I said. "Imagine what other information Ursula might be recording using that spell? She's breaking the law."

Estelle's mouth pinched. "You're right. I'll see if that's enough for Edwin to arrest *her.*"

We returned to the library, where we found Aunt Adelaide pacing the lobby with a scowl on her face.

"There you are," she said. "Nobody confessed, and none of the other patrons have the skills or reasons to use the curse. They don't know who Ursula is, either. What took you so long?"

"Gareth," I said. "He worked with Ursula to bug the

library with a recording spell in order to spy on us. He confessed to the police."

"But he didn't admit to setting off the curse," added Estelle. "He got caught in the wand shop when he tried to bug the place, too. Guess Ursula wanted to interview them about the Magpie."

"I still don't think it's a coincidence that she arrived in town at the same time as the thief did," I said. "Perhaps *that's* the story she was searching for."

"It's irrelevant," said Aunt Adelaide tightly. "The thief hasn't stolen anything from us, so there's no connection."

My stomach sank. "Are you sure nothing's gone missing lately?"

Estelle eyed me curiously. "Like what?"

I turned to my aunt. "Aunt Adelaide, do you know where the book for the forbidden room is? I tried asking Sylvester earlier, but he's missing."

She frowned. "No, I can't keep track of anything in here, not since the gravity spell. What do you need that for? You haven't been into that room, have you?"

Oh, no. It had totally slipped my mind that I hadn't told her about my first expedition into the forbidden room.

"Um, once or twice," I said. "It's how we found Cass when the vampires' killer took her..."

Aunt Adelaide's mouth pressed together. "Far be it from me to treat you like a child, Rory, but that room isn't intended for beginner witches. Granted, there were extenuating circumstances, but in a case such as this one, we ought to be able to find the spell's cause without needing to consult the room."

"I know, but it's missing." It was hardly the only book

to disappear, but my aunt didn't know about Sylvester's link with the forbidden room. Nobody knew aside from me, in fact.

Aunt Adelaide sighed. "Can you look for the eavesdropping spell instead? It's imperative that we get any traces of Ursula out of the library. If we can get *her* locked up for lawbreaking, so much the better."

She swept away, leaving me alone with Estelle.

"The front desk," she said. "That's where he said he left the spell, but the place has been rearranged a dozen times this week alone."

"I know." I walked to join her at the front of the library. "The question room would be able to find the eavesdropping spell in a second, but the book is nowhere around. Are you sure Ursula didn't take anything when she came into the library?"

"I was watching her the whole time," she said. "No, I don't think she did. And as useful as that room is, Rory, we're lucky we got out in one piece last time. We don't want to push our luck. My mum's right… that room isn't for casual use."

"I know," I said. "I just—I tried to ask Sylvester to find it and he wouldn't answer. Has anyone seen him since the party?"

"Sylvester's been disappearing all week, Rory," said Estelle. "I never expect him to show up when we need him. He works for himself, and he's never been shy about expressing it."

No... he works for the library. But with the book *and* the owl gone, his disappearance seemed more suspicious by the second. And the person who'd set off the curse would have reason to ensure Sylvester didn't get in their way.

"He'll turn up," added Estelle. "I'm more concerned that he might not have a library to come back to."

No kidding. If Ursula got away with claiming her innocence and her story made it to print, we might lose the library. Forever.

12

I woke late the next day, having spent half the night thumbing through copies of Aunt Candace's books. While rampaging elves and horses weren't the worst of what we'd seen this week, the pile of books on the coffee table in the back room was a reminder that we'd barely scratched the surface of Aunt Candace's extensive back catalogue. I'd eventually dozed off with my head pillowed on the open copy of my dad's life story. I moved my head and it fell to the floor with a thump. Yawning, I rolled onto my side, opening my eyes.

I wasn't in my bedroom, but back in my old apartment. The second-hand furniture, the work clothes lying ready on the back of the chair, dull-coloured blouses and long skirts and cardigans were in the same place they'd been before I'd moved to the library. Even my books were in their old shelves beside my bed.

Impossible. Once I'd moved all my possessions to the library, I'd left that world behind. Someone else had moved into my flat, and no traces of my former life remained. Yet the flat looked as real as I was.

"I can't have dreamt it all." My voice echoed in the empty room, which seemed smaller than it had before I'd set foot in the library. "And this can't be the curse, either. Aunt Candace has never written my old apartment into a book." At least, I didn't *think* she had. I'd be having words with her if she'd turned out to be writing *my* life story as a follow-up to my dad's.

Speaking of which… I reached under my head and found the copy of Aunt Candace's book I'd fallen asleep reading. *That* was real.

So was everything else just a dream?

I shoved the thought aside. I might have a vivid imagination, but there was no way I could dream up anything as wondrous as my experiences since I'd moved to the library. No, *this* was the dream. It wasn't the first time I'd revisited the memories of my former life, and I *had* fallen asleep in the middle of reading my dad's life story. It was no wonder the past was in the forefront of my mind.

I ignored the old clothes, the second-hand furniture, and opened the door. Instead of a corridor, I found myself in the landing of the old house Dad and I had lived in before his death.

I stared at the beige wallpaper and the navy carpets, now thoroughly baffled. I'd moved out of the house a month after Dad had passed away. Unable to deal with living in his home without him there, I'd taken the money he'd left me and put down a deposit on my flat. Last I'd heard, another family had moved into our old house years ago.

"I'd like to wake up now," I said to the world at large. "Please."

I didn't expect an answer, much less what happened next.

"Rory?" said a familiar voice. "Is that you?"

Common sense flew out the window as a stair creaked, then another. I remained still as an achingly familiar face came into view…

Dad.

I gasped aloud. Then I ran and hugged him, tightly. He hugged me back, and tears clogged my throat. He felt real. So real.

"You're okay," I said. "You're alive."

"Rory, what's wrong?" he asked. "Of course I'm okay. I just went to the library to see if it was okay to bring the others to meet you."

"To visit who?" I wiped my eyes with the back of my hand. Then I stared.

Aunt Adelaide and Aunt Candace stood behind him, both beaming. At Aunt Adelaide's side stood her ex-husband, along with Cass and Estelle.

"How is this possible?" I asked. "I thought telling normals about the magical world was forbidden."

"But we aren't normals, are we?" he said. "We're biblio-witches."

"Some of us are normals," said a female voice.

A woman appeared at his side, smiling, her hair bouncing to her shoulders the way it had when she was alive.

Mum.

"You're…" *Not real.* But they *looked* real. As real as the library. "You're alive, too. Why—why didn't you tell me?"

Mum took both my hands. As though it hadn't had been fifteen years since she'd touched me. "We're normals, Rory. We don't belong here."

"I do." My voice sounded small, and when I let go of her hands, tears fell down my cheeks. "I know this isn't real. None of this is. I want to wake up—*now.*"

I turned my back on my family and found myself faced with the ground floor of the library, looking very much like it always did. I stepped forwards, my feet sinking into the soft carpet. *Is everything I see an illusion? I know I'm awake—so how do I get out?*

Footsteps came from behind me, followed by the sound of a door opening. I spun on the spot and found my flat, and the old house, had vanished. So had the others, except for Aunt Adelaide, who looked up as Dad entered the library.

"There you are, Roger," she said, accosting him. "I was beginning to think you'd never come back."

I looked between them, my heart sinking. *It's still not real.* And neither of them looked at me. In fact, their words sounded... familiar.

"Of course I did," Dad said, a second too late. That second-long pause said it all. He had something he needed to say, but was worried about his sister's reaction.

I know this. I read *this.*

"You've been downright careless," said Aunt Adelaide. "Fancy leaving your wand behind—and that Maurice kid tried to steal it again. You know that was a mistake."

"I didn't come back to be reminded of all my youthful mistakes." Dad sounded tired. Probably because he'd been on a long train journey to get back here, without his wand.

"First you lose your wand, then you lose your heart," said Aunt Candace. "To a normal, at that."

"I didn't lose my wand," he retaliated. "It's right here where I left it. As for my heart, I gave it away by choice."

Aunt Candace mimed vomiting behind the desk.

A hand grabbed mine, and I screamed.

"Whoa." Xavier. I spun around when he let go of my hand. He blinked at me with a bemused expression on his face, looking out of place in this new, faded version of the library.

Then I looked down at myself. I was not, as I'd thought, wearing my cloak. I was in my pyjamas.

"Oh god, I really am dreaming," I said. "Or having a nightmare."

"Do I often appear in your dreams?" asked Xavier. "Sorry for startling you."

Ack. "If this isn't a dream, how did you get into the library? This is supposed to be an illusion. I mean, it must be. That's my dad." I waved a hand towards him and my aunts, none of whom had looked up at his sudden appearance.

"Wait, that's your dad?" he asked. "Of course... he looks just like you."

"You can see him, too?" I rubbed my damp eyes. "How?"

"You don't really believe you're dreaming, do you?" He smiled. "Because as flattering as it might be to imagine I'm starring in your dream, you look a little freaked out."

"Because my dad is standing right there," I said. "Please tell me I'm not standing here talking to you in my pyjamas while an illusion of my dead father has a chat with my aunts."

"Okay, I won't tell you," he said, his voice light, teasing. I fought the impulse to grab him to make sure he felt as real as he sounded. My mum had felt like a real person, too, after all. Yet she'd vanished from sight. All that remained was the library, Xavier, and an all-too-familiar scene playing out before my eyes. Because I'd read it in my aunt's book before I'd fallen asleep.

Dad's voice rose in volume. "I love her. Don't force me to choose, Adelaide. I care for both of you, too."

"He's talking about your mother?" Xavier guessed. "What is this—a memory?"

"Not mine," I said. "I guess this is the next stage of the Manifestation Curse—the epic love story between my parents. I wasn't even born yet."

He stared at them. "Your aunt wrote your life story into a book?"

"How are you the only person in town who *doesn't* know that? It's the one book she published under her real name. Dedicated to me, under the name 'the lost cousin'. I don't know why she did that, considering she knew my name, *and* I'm not her cousin—"

"Be reasonable, Roger," said Aunt Adelaide. "You brought Maurice here, at great risk, and you should know better than to consider bringing another normal into our world. They just don't belong here."

"This is different," he insisted. "I love her, and she loves me. She's willing to make it work. Not that I've told her about the library yet, of course."

"I'm glad you've learned," said Grandma. "Really, Roger, I thought your days of rule-breaking were over. Maurice was never the same afterwards. Foolish boy."

I stood stock-still. *Dad brought someone else here before Mum? A normal? They came into the magical world?*

Or was Aunt Candace making the whole thing up for drama? I had no way of knowing without the real people to question. Granted, my dad had given her permission to write the book, but that didn't mean she couldn't let her imagination run riot over the pages.

"What's she talking about?" Xavier asked.

"I have no idea," I said. "I fell asleep before I got to this part of the story. I'm not sure if that's really Aunt Adelaide, bewitched to think it's twenty-something years ago, or if it's just an illusion. Why'd you come here, anyway?"

"I was worried about you," he said. "I heard the vampires' leader paid you a visit."

I'd forgotten all about Evangeline's offer. "Yeah, she tried to persuade me to trade my dad's journal for information on how to undo the curse. I refused, but maybe I shouldn't have. We can't prove Ursula's guilt, and the other guy we suspected turned out to be a false lead, too."

"Hang on, who?" he said.

I explained our ongoing feud with Ursula, and our discovery that Gareth had bugged the library at her request.

"Not that I have the slightest chance of finding a recording spell in here with the past replaying in front of my eyes," I said. "It might be anywhere. And I don't know if it can record illusions like this, but she knows something's wrong at the library and she has enough material to write a month's worth of scathing articles on us by now."

"But she didn't start this? Or do you think she paid

someone else to cast the curse and then planted the book in the library?"

"That's what I thought at first," I said. "Now I don't know what to think. Either she had another accomplice, or someone is playing all of us."

I glanced back at the others, who continued to act out a pre-determined series of events as though they didn't have a real, live family member watching them from the side-lines.

Xavier's brow furrowed. "They can't be your aunts. Otherwise, who's your dad?"

"An illusion." A lump lodged in my throat. "This is the story of how he met Mum and was forced to leave the magical world behind. That's why I didn't know about any of this until my magic awakened."

So many things had changed that day. Me, most of all. Yet seeing a whole world I'd never experience… seeing my dad whole, happy, without me… I had to get out of here, before I lost my mind, swept up in visions of the past.

"Oh, Rory?" said Aunt Candace.

My heart jumped into my throat. "You can see me?"

"Good name, isn't it?" Aunt Candace went on, as though I hadn't spoken.

"I like it," said Dad. "It sounds fierce."

"She won't be fierce," said Aunt Candace. "She'll be a softy like you, I'll bet."

She named me? No way. She'd probably fictionalised the events to make herself the hero. At least *that* was a clear reminder I was watching a replay of the book's events—not the past as it had actually happened.

"This is beyond weird," I muttered. "I guess this is when he told them my mum was having me."

"You can't say a word to her," said Aunt Adelaide. "What are you going to do with the wand, then? You can't take it with you."

"I know," he said. "I'll leave it here in the library, just in case."

"Are you sure?" Aunt Adelaide's head was bowed. "Is this your final decision—renounce the magical world altogether?"

Dad put his hand in his pocket and removed a small black book. I held back a gasp. He was giving her his Biblio-Witch Inventory. Then his pen, notebook, and finally, his wand.

"Take care of them for me," he said. "In case I decide to come back."

"We know you're not coming back, Roger," said Aunt Adelaide.

Unable to watch another second, I dragged my gaze away.

Xavier's arm wrapped around my shoulder. "It's not real."

"I know." I blinked hard. "It's my aunt's interpretation of events, too, so she's bound to have changed things to make them more dramatic. Maybe it'd be less jarring if I'd finished reading the book first."

Dad paused beside the door and turned back. He looked up at the library, his expression a mixture of sorrow, regret, determination, and so much more. My heart seized. If not for me, he'd have been able to come back after Mum died, to return to his old life. Yet he'd stayed out there in the real world, working in that dismal shop with Abe, just for my sake. He'd left his wand behind, hadn't even used it to save his own life.

I shook my head. "I'm going to find... find some clothes. Assuming my room even still exists in this reality."

"I'll be waiting right here," Xavier said.

Nodding thanks, I walked towards the family's living quarters, but it wasn't there. Instead, a blank wall stood in its place. The whole library had changed. This must be what it had looked like before my dad had left, and I hadn't a clue where the family's living quarters might be. Perhaps my room wasn't here at all.

All right, let's do it this way, then.

I pulled out my notebook, and wrote, *clothes.* I fixed the image in my head as strongly as possible, concentrating on the magic and not on the scene playing out in the library.

Then I looked down to see I was fully dressed. At least my magic still worked in this version of reality, even if I didn't exist.

I walked back to join Xavier by the desk, which was more neatly arranged than it'd been all week. None of the books looked like they might hide a recording spell. Wait —did the book of questions exist in this reality? I peered under the desk, but found nothing but dust. Everything was shelved away.

"What're you looking for?" asked Xavier.

"The eavesdropping spell Gareth left in a book here," I said. "And the book of questions. I think it's missing, and that the person who cast the curse took it."

"Missing?" he said. "Didn't all the books in the library move around when gravity turned off?"

"They did," I said. "But the book of questions might be able to tell me how to undo this curse, or at least find the culprit. I can't believe Ursula seems to be innocent. Unless we find her real accomplice."

"Have you told the police your suspicions?" he asked.

"I have, but Ursula wasn't in the library when the curse went off, and she has an alibi," I said. "As for the copy of *The Adventures of Werewolves in Cyberland* that started all this, if we can't figure out who planted it in the library, we can't prove she put them up to it. Gareth admitted to planting a recording spell, but there's a world of difference between that and a curse. And I can't find either of them with everything stuck in the past."

"True," he acknowledged. "Then we'll go to speak to Edwin again. If you tell him your entire family is caught up in the spell—"

"Then Ursula will get the story she wants. We might even get shut down." A lump formed in my throat. I couldn't lose the library *or* my family.

"That won't happen," he said. "Edwin knows better than to give her any more stories to print."

"You shouldn't stay here with me," I said. "Your boss will give you hell when he finds out you're helping me instead of doing your job."

"I'll risk it," he said.

I shook my head. "I know you don't remember the other night, but I do, and—he was really mad at you."

"You think I don't remember?" he said. "Rory—I do remember."

My heart gave a painful thump. Did he mean… did he mean he *hadn't* entirely been under the spell's influence?

"You do?"

"I do," he said. "I didn't notice anything was wrong. I should have checked the list of souls to collect, but I couldn't sense them the way I normally would. My attention was on the library and on you."

"So... you didn't drink the champagne?"

"Reaper, remember? Nothing like that affects me."

"The curse did." I clamped my mouth shut, too late.

"I suppose it did," he said. "But maybe I wanted to be there. I haven't had so much fun in a long time. I didn't care what the Reaper said. And I don't care now."

He did enjoy it. Spell or not.

Emotions hit me in a rush, and I wrapped my arms around him. He hugged me, reassuringly solid for an angel of death.

Then he released me. "We'll get to the bottom of this, Rory."

To my relief, the world outside the library looked no different than usual, from the slate-grey sky to the crowds of shoppers. But would it last? Or would the curse continue to spread until the fictional world replaced the real one?

I walked with Xavier, the chill wind biting at my exposed face and hands. For once, I didn't mind how cold it was. At least I knew it was real.

We reached the seafront and made our way into the police station. Edwin's brows rose at the sight of Xavier. "Is there something I can help you with, Reaper?"

"I hope so," Xavier said. "Rory's family is affected by the curse—"

"Not this curse again," he said, sounding annoyed. "I told you not to—"

The phone rang loudly. Edwin released a breath and then picked it up. "Yes?"

He listened, and his expression grew more and more serious with each passing second. Then he hung up.

"It seems Mr Hale from the wand shop was murdered this morning."

I clapped a hand to my mouth. "No."

"Sadly, yes," he said. "Did you know him?"

"I spoke to him just yesterday." Who could have killed him? Except—

"Isn't Gareth here?" asked Xavier. "He tried to break into the wand shop yesterday."

"I'm aware of that," said Edwin. "He's locked in his cell, and he's been there all night."

"He was acting on Ursula's orders," I said. "He confessed to it, as you heard. *She* wasn't in jail, was she?"

Edwin looked between us. "I will call her here for questioning, then."

13

Xavier and I waited in the police station for at least an hour before Edwin returned. The Reaper was content to talk to the troll guards amiably, but I was restless. My family were trapped in the library, an innocent man had died, and now… now we might be about to catch the culprit, yet I still felt like I was missing something major.

I'd made the right call, hadn't I? Ursula was the one person connected to all the parts of the curse. She also had an incentive—more than one—to hurt my family. Not to mention, she and the thief had arrived in town around the same time, right before the curse had activated. Yet despite all that, it was hard to picture her as a murderer.

I stopped pacing beside Edwin's desk, my gaze snagging on the photos on the wall. Each image looked slightly different, as though the Magpie was changing his appearance with each incarnation—and yet in the most close-up images, I was sure I *did* know him. *It can't be.*

I dug in my bag, and the door opened. Edwin walked

in, followed by Ursula. She looked as polished as ever, but despite her well-coiled hair and expertly-applied makeup, hints of worry showed in her features. "What is the meaning of this?"

"A man is dead," said Edwin. "Since you're already accused of being connected with several other crimes, I saw fit to bring you here for questioning."

"I did no such thing," she insisted. "Candace has been out to get me since we were students together."

"Gareth has already confessed to helping you illegally bug locations in town in order to spy on the residents," he said. "The owner of one of those places, the wand shop, was found dead this morning."

From the shock on her face, I would have been certain she hadn't known—if I didn't know how good a liar she was, anyway. She let Edwin and the trolls steer her into the same room we'd questioned Gareth in, and sank into the chair.

"What's she doing here?" Ursula asked, catching sight of me. "Did she put you up to this?"

"No." I pulled out the copy of *The Adventures of Werewolves in Cyberland*. "This is the book that caused the Manifestation Curse which started in the library this week. It's getting worse, and only the caster can take off the spell. All the signs point to Ursula being the person responsible for the curse, since the book is signed and addressed to her."

Ursula looked from the book to me, her mouth twisting. "Fine. I'll explain everything."

"Do so." Edwin looked expectantly at her.

Her shoulders slumped. "Mr Hale refused to speak with me, so I asked Gareth to find a way of obtaining the information I needed for my article. If someone murdered him, it had no connection with my actions. If Gareth has been locked up the whole time, he can't have committed the murder, can he?"

"You're forgetting the part where you had him plant a recording spell in the library to spy on us," I said. "*This* book is the spell, isn't it? It's been listening in on our conversations all along."

Her lip curled. "Yes, very clever. Will that convince you that I had nothing to do with the curse someone used on your family?"

"No. The book might be cursed as well as planted with a recording spell. The first book that came to life under the curse had this exact title, and it's the only copy of the book we found in the library."

"She's right," Xavier added. "If I fetch the curse-breaker, will he back up what you say?"

"Of course." Her voice trembled a little. "I had nothing to do with the curse, *or* Mr Hale's death."

"Then I'll ask Mr Bennet." Xavier retreated, while I remained standing awkwardly beside the troll guards. *The curse-breaker can't refuse to examine the book in front of witnesses.* But the presence of the thief's photos was a reminder that there were still several parts of this which went unexplained.

While Xavier was gone, I turned to Ursula. "You said you came here for a story," I said. "How'd you know you'd find one if you didn't engineer the curse yourself?"

"Because your family leaves drama wherever they tread," she said.

"So you had a particular interest in Rory's family?" Edwin watched her with obvious dislike. *He's on our side.*

Lucky for us—and yet my family remained trapped in the curse. "Because of their position in the library?"

"Or because of my dad?" I frowned at her. "Why the wand shop, then? Are you really so interested in whether I get a wand or not?"

"It's not about you, Aurora," she said.

I folded my arms. "Then who? The rest of my family has had wands for their whole lives. I'm the only one of us who's moved here recently."

"That's not—" She broke off as the front door opened. Xavier glided into the room a moment later, followed by the curse-breaker. "Mr Bennet. You refused to provide me with an interview."

He did? Odd. He was one of the few people in town who *did* have reason to dislike my family, thanks to his lingering grudge against my grandmother.

"I did," he confirmed. "Where is this book?"

"Here." I handed him the book, more confused than ever. "It's jinxed with an eavesdropping spell, isn't it?"

He held the book for a moment, turning it over in his hands. "Yes, it is. Nothing more, just a simple eavesdropping charm."

My heart sank. The book wasn't the source of the curse. But if Gareth had planted it in the library without cursing it... *which* book was cursed, and where was it now?

Ursula shifted in her seat. "So you admit I'm innocent? I expect an apology."

"You're not off the hook," I said. "You spied on us behind our backs, not to mention sending Gareth to steal from the wand shop. You still broke the law, even if you aren't the killer."

"Yes, and she will be punished accordingly." Edwin waved a hand, dismissing us. "Watch her. I will see the others out."

"Is that all?" said Mr Bennet, walking out into the lobby.

"Can't—I mean, can you tell where the curse might be coming from?" I asked desperately. "It was cast on this particular title, but there must be another copy somewhere in the library."

"I'm afraid I cannot help you unless the source is found," he said. "And even then, the caster must undo it. Soon. The curse is spreading, and in cases like this, the curse will eventually start to displace reality. The entire town might fall under its spell."

I gasped. "But—the town in the book isn't an exact mirror of reality. She made up people and created fake names to avoid lawsuits. The Reaper wasn't involved in the book, for one. He can't just disappear."

"He'll probably be fine," said Mr Bennet. "Since he doesn't belong to the same plane as the rest of you."

"Doesn't belong to the same...?" I trailed off. "Because there can't be a world without a Reaper."

But me? My family? We might all disappear. Or turn into the previous versions of ourselves from the lives we'd had before I'd ever moved here.

I *couldn't* go back to being that person again. I couldn't lose my family.

Mr Bennet left the police station. Xavier made to follow, but I didn't move.

"I think he did it," I said quietly.

Xavier turned back. "Rory? Who did what?"

"The thief was the person who set off the curse. I don't know *why,* though."

To steal from us? But then, what was his interest in the library to begin with? Unless *he'd* been the one to take the book of questions, but how would he even know it existed?

"So who planted the book in the library and why?" Edwin asked from behind me.

"To set off the curse… and create a diversion," I said. "I'm sure of it."

He blinked. "How do you know?"

"I don't, but I can find proof." *I think.* I needed to speak to my aunts to confirm my suspicions, assuming they weren't incapable of communicating, doomed to replay the events of my dad's life story forever.

I hurried out of the police station, Xavier on my heels, leaving a bewildered Edwin behind us.

"You're sure your family is in there somewhere?" he asked.

"They must be." I quickened my pace, heading for the town square. "Cass and Estelle weren't born when my parents met, so I don't understand why they disappeared and I didn't."

"Because you're not part of the story?"

I wasn't part of their narrative. I was just the lost cousin in this version of the world.

And it was only a matter of time before I disappeared from existence.

No. I won't let that happen. I'll stop this first.

"They're alive," I said, with more confidence than I really felt. "Even Mum is, in this reality. I wouldn't have thought Aunt Candace would have written Mum's death from cancer in the book, if it was an epic romance."

"It was?" he said. "So the book is essentially about your father meeting your mother, falling in love, and then leaving the library behind? Does it show what happened afterwards, or is that it?"

"Pretty much," I said. "Afterwards, the library threw a tantrum and went into complete chaos, or so I'm told. It's possible that the thief knew that was going to happen..."

"Maybe." He frowned, his brow crinkling. "If it's not personal, then how would the thief have known that was going to happen today?"

"Fair point," I said. "I think the curse was just a diversion, but... I don't know. I need to talk to my aunts."

"But why did he need a curse that big just for a diversion?"

"Because he wanted to steal something big?"

Or—

Or the thief was already in the library. He'd never left.

A shadow fell across the square, and the Grim Reaper stepped onto the path in front of us.

My heart jumped into my throat.

Waves of silence rippled across the square. Nobody else was around, either because of the curse or because the Grim Reaper's presence had sent them fleeing.

He looked me up and down. "Aurora Hawthorn. What exactly are you doing with my apprentice?"

"Nothing," I said, far too quickly. At least I knew I wasn't dreaming. No spell could manifest an exact image of the terrifying Grim Reaper. He was beyond reality, and no curse could banish *him* from existence. Pity I couldn't say the same for the rest of us.

"I came to help Rory with the curse," Xavier said. "Her family has fallen under the effects of the curse. Considering the curse affects the nature of reality, I'm concerned it will affect my ability to do my job."

"My cousins have both gone missing in the library," I hastened to add. "And my aunts are trapped under the spell. Xavier came to check on me and help me report the incident to the police. The thief—he was responsible for the curse, and I think he's still in there."

"Then you had better go back to the library," he said coldly. "Come, Xavier."

No. I can't lose my only ally.

Pleading looks were lost on the Grim Reaper, and as he beckoned again, Xavier stepped after him. He gave me a last apologetic look, and was gone.

I can't dwell on him. I was the only person who could get my family back, and if I hesitated, I might never see them again.

Sucking in a deep breath, I pushed open the door to the library.

It was as though the anti-gravity effects had switched on again, combined with the décor Aunt Candace had once conjured up when Dominic had died. Black drapes covered everything, while the books spun in circles, making me dizzy. Serve me right for bringing up the subject—this was the state of the library after my dad had left it forever.

I ducked through the rows of spinning books, arms over my head to shield myself. "This isn't real," I said. "This isn't—"

A book hit me full in the face, making sparks dance before my eyes. Ow. That *felt* real.

I sucked in a deep breath and called out. "Hey, Aunt Adelaide! Aunt Candace! Where are you?"

Silence responded. My fear grew, and so did my resolve. "Okay, thief. I know you're in here. I think I know who you are, too, but I don't understand why you hate my family so much—"

Another book clipped the side of my face. Rows of them spun like a merry-go-round, forming a whirling dervish that filled half the reception area. If anyone tried to walk in, they'd get bombarded.

Think, Rory. I dug in my bag, but what use was basic biblio-witch magic against a curse this powerful? I needed more than that.

My hand brushed against the emergency paper in the bottom of my pocket. If any situation constituted an emergency, it was this one.

That's if it works when my aunts are under a curse.

"One way to find out." I tapped the word *help.*

The library kept on spinning. Then Aunt Adelaide and Aunt Candace tumbled into the middle of the lobby in a heap. Aunt Candace yelped and shielded her face from the whirling books, while Aunt Adelaide straightened upright, pulling out her Biblio-Witch Inventory. She tapped a word, and the books flew backwards, but didn't return to their shelves.

"You're alive!" I exclaimed. "Please tell me you can see me."

"I can hear you, too," grumbled Aunt Candace. "I'm too old for this."

I sagged against the desk with relief. "I thought you were going to be stuck under the curse forever."

"It won't last," Aunt Adelaide said. "The emergency

button creates a loophole, but the whole library is under the curse. And when it spreads—"

"It'll reach the whole town. I know." I dug in my bag for my copy of *Entranced by the Normal*. "This is what's replaying. Who is the man in the photograph?"

Aunt Adelaide's eyes widened as I held it up. "Maurice Hudson. A friend of your dad's. I didn't know there were any photos left."

"Except for the wedding photo," I went on. "He was the best man."

"Yes..."

"And he was a normal."

A book flew past, and Aunt Adelaide smacked it out of the way. "Yes, but I don't see how this is relevant—"

"It's him." I had to raise my voice over the clamour of moving shelves. "He's doing this. I don't know if it's revenge or whatever, but I've seen photos of the thief and it's definitely him. I don't know how he turned out to have magic after all, either but I think he came here for revenge—and he killed Mr Hale from the wand shop."

Aunt Adelaide clapped her hands to her mouth, while Aunt Candace swore. "I knew there was something not quite right about that boy."

"And he's in here," I pressed. "Look—the thief is *here* in the library. He never left. And he set off the curse, so—"

"He didn't," Aunt Candace interrupted. "That is—he *did,* but the Manifestation Curse was mine. Your father and I made it together."

Aunt Adelaide stared at her. "You *what?*"

She shrugged, looking embarrassed. "It was Roger's idea. When we were teenagers, we thought it amusing to see if we could make a biblio-witch spell that would bring fantasies to life. We thought it would be fun entertainment for the locals—controlled, of course. It was supposed to be contained within a single room. But we couldn't get it to stay under control. And the prototype… I thought I lost it somewhere up on the third floor."

"So the thief found it?" I said. "And I guess one of you told him about it. Just like you told him about the forbidden book."

Aunt Adelaide looked alarmed. "Candace, please tell me you didn't."

"We were children," she said defensively. "Has a normal ever bested a witch before?"

"Look at the state of the place," she said, waving a hand. "We have only a short time before the curse sucks us in again, and—"

"And the thief is hiding in here somewhere," I added.

"The curse doesn't affect you, Rory," said Aunt Candace. "Perhaps it's because the affected books were written before you moved here. I'll have to look into it afterwards."

"If there *is* an afterwards," said Aunt Adelaide. The spinning books gained speed, while the lobby began to warp before my eyes.

Then, in an instant, my aunts were gone.

I sank to the carpet. *I can't do this. I'm not a worthy biblio-witch.* I couldn't even use a wand.

But if I didn't find a way to undo the curse, my family would lose everything. Even Dad would lose the life he'd wanted me to have. The reason he'd asked for Aunt Candace to write the book and dedicate it to me. The lost cousin. No longer lost, now I had a home.

The book fell to the floor where Aunt Adelaide had dropped it. *The lost cousin,* the dedication read.

Dad had believed in me, and I would make him proud. I'd save the library he'd loved so much, even if it meant losing him again.

14

I walked through the library, hoping it wouldn't be the last time. While the spinning had stopped, my aunts remained in the lobby, playing out the same scenes over and over again.

I ignored them. I had to find the thief before it was too late. Didn't mean I had to do it alone, though. If I didn't exist in this universe, maybe my familiar didn't either.

"Jet," I said. "I need you."

"Partner!" squeaked Jet, landing on my shoulder. "It's not safe in here!"

"I know that," I said. "But I have to help the others."

I pulled out my Biblio-Witch Inventory, treading through the stacks towards the stairs. I couldn't think of anywhere to look except for where it all started—up on the third floor. The thief had a whole library to hide in, but if he'd taken the book of questions, that must still be in here, too. With him.

Calling for Sylvester didn't work, as I'd expected, but at least I had my own familiar ready to help. I climbed the stairs, my heart pounding in my ears. The library grew darker as I climbed, which didn't help my growing apprehension. Just what kind of powers did the Magpie have? How had he turned out to be magical when he hadn't been able to claim a wand when he'd first tried to enter the paranormal world?

More to the point, how had he got in here without any of us noticing? The library's defences repelled anyone who intended harm, but perhaps the curse was too subtle to be detected. It explained how he'd managed to sneak around town committing robberies without being caught, since the library was easy to hide in even when it wasn't under a curse. I'd bet he'd slipped outside to rob the bank during the party, then crept back inside again with the other guests.

And now Mr Hale was dead. Murdered, because of all the people in Ivory Beach, he was most likely to work out the thief's true identity. It had been Mr Hale who'd tried to sell him a wand all those years ago, after all.

He's a madman, and I'm off to confront him alone. Higher and higher I climbed, and the darkness deepened until I was forced to tap the word *light* in my Biblio-Witch Inventory. The light put a beacon on my head, but it was that or fall downstairs.

Jet shifted on my shoulder. "It's dark, partner."

"I know." I winced when his claws dug into the skin of my neck. "Don't worry. If the curse keeps cycling through all Aunt Candace's books, there isn't anything in here that we haven't seen before. I know what's real and what isn't."

My feet touched down on the third floor. It was pitch black, with a horrible smell lingering in the air. Had Cass's manticore got out again?

Holding my Biblio-Witch Inventory in shaking hands, I tapped the word *light* and it ignited like a torch, showing me the huge shape of the manticore towering over my head, jaws slavering.

"Hi." My throat went dry. "Let you out of your cage, did he?"

The manticore, which resembled a cross between a giant lobster and a lion, roared, snapping its pincers. I jumped behind the nearest shelf, jabbing at the page and hitting the word *rise.* My spell missed and hit the bookcase, which flew into the air, dislodging hardbacks. Backing away, I found myself trapped between two sides of towering shelves.

Not shelves. Trees, with thick trunks and grasping branches. I backed up further, and the trees thickened, branches rustling.

Oh, no. I'd skimmed Aunt Candace's horror pen name's books last night and I was pretty sure one had involved a monster stalking people in the woods. I'd prefer not to find out the hard way if it was possible to die in an enactment of a fictional tale.

The manticore roared from the other side of the shelves, its pincers knocking the books aside. With a loud caw, Jet flew around the manticore's head, his tiny feathered shape distracting the monster from its human prey. I ran out of the 'forest' and into a maze of bookshelves, my heart pounding. As long as I held the light, the beast would be able to track me, but without it, I'd be lost in darkness.

I ran down the nearest row of shelves, finding myself backed up against the far wall. The only way out was through the door into the Magical Creatures Division—

the same place the manticore had escaped from. At least I knew its cage was empty.

Pelting behind the door, I slammed it closed, and then darted into the manticore's empty room. Now I'd backed myself into a corner, but what choice did I have? The manticore wasn't tame even when it wasn't acting out one of Aunt Candace's horror stories. If I ever got out of this alive, I'd order her to destroy all evidence of the Manifestation Curse or else I'd throw all her horror pen name's books into the ocean.

With shaking hands, I wrote the word *lock* in my notebook, willing the door to hold closed.

Please be okay, Jet.

The manticore's growls grew closer, and I edged backwards until I was right in front of the empty cage. Tattered pages littered the floor, suggesting the beast had snacked on a book recently. The word *werewolf* stood out on one page. Hang on a second.

I spun on the spot, scanning the other scattered pages. Sure enough, among them lay the tattered remains of the cover of *The Adventures of Werewolves in Cyberland.* The manticore had chewed up the whole book—the perfect way to dispose of the evidence. I didn't particularly want to pick up the slimy remains of the cover, covered in the manticore's drool, but only Aunt Candace could undo the curse, which meant getting hold of the book was only half the battle.

The door trembled against its hinges, and the manticore let out a deafening roar. *Oh, god.*

It didn't matter where the thief was now—I was trapped in a manticore's cage, and the curse had taken on a life of its own, escaping the book altogether.

"Is that it?" I said loudly. "Are you going to let the manticore eat me without showing your face? I know who you are, Maurice. I know you wanted to make my dad and his family sorry for the way the magical world rejected you. I would have thought you'd want to speak to me yourself rather than letting the manticore do the talking, considering I have what you always wanted and never managed to gain."

Silence. The door didn't tremble again. I held my breath, gripping my pen and notebook. At my feet, the shredded remains of Aunt Candace's novel lay scattered in piles covered in serrated tooth marks.

Then a voice called back, "You won't make it out alive, Aurora, one way or another."

"I thought you were friends." My voice shook. "You and my dad. He never meant you any harm."

"He mocked me," he said. "He brought me here to this town, only to let his people cast me out. He even threatened to erase my memories."

"Maybe he should have." My heart thumped erratically. "He broke the law to bring you here. He was only trying to help a friend. It's not his fault the magical world didn't accept you. And I wasn't even born at the time, so punishing me will achieve nothing."

"He *gave it all up for you."*

The door flew open and I braced myself, but it wasn't the manticore who greeted me. Instead, the man from the photographs—the man who'd been at Mum and Dad's wedding—stood there. Tall and thin, with dark hair, his narrow face identical to the photographs of the Magpie beside Edwin's desk.

"I don't understand what you—"

"He *gave it up.* All this." He gave a sweeping gesture at the library in general. "He turned his back and walked away, as though he didn't have a choice. Like I didn't."

"That doesn't make it my fault." The notebook's spine dug into my hand.

"You're nothing more than a pretender, Aurora Hawthorn," he said. "You're a normal, and you never should have been allowed to come here."

"So because the magical world didn't accept you, you decided to target me instead of my dad?" I said. "It wasn't my fault any more than it was my dad's. I'm sorry you didn't get the wand you wanted, but that's no excuse to commit murder."

Maurice flinched. "That old wand-maker wasn't supposed to see me. I couldn't let him go blabbing to the police and that nosy reporter."

"You stole from him," I said. "You stole the book of questions, too, didn't you? Let me guess... that didn't work for you either."

And he'd either caught Sylvester or the owl had taken refuge inside the book to avoid him. Those signatures he left at the crime scenes had seemed to be proof he was a wizard, but nobody had ever seen him leave one. For all his legendary crimes, he'd never been seen using magic. Because he couldn't.

"Don't you dare mock me." His mouth twisted. "Your family has hoarded the magic of the biblio-witches for long enough. Now it's time to take what Roger denied me. He chose to give up his magic, so I will take it back."

He wants Dad's wand. Dad had given it up, along with his Biblio-Witch Inventory, when he'd left town—abandoning both of them here in the library. "You can't take a wand from someone else. Even a witch or wizard can't."

"There *is* a way." He held up the book of questions. "I want you to go into that room and find out what it is, Aurora Hawthorn. Or you'll never see your family again."

15

I stood rigid, both eyes on the book of questions. Sylvester would help me if he could, but Maurice wouldn't stop with Dad's wand—and even if I found it, no spell would make it obey him like a real wizard. No matter what happened, he'd take it out on my family.

"I can't," I said. "You aren't entitled to steal something that isn't yours. I don't even know where the wand is."

"Pity," he said. "I won't let you leave this library until you give me what I need."

He's mad. Mad with jealousy—and I knew with certainty that if Dad was anything like me, he'd have blamed himself for bringing Maurice into the library to begin with. Even though there was no way he could have known his friend would react so badly to not turning out to be magical. I could put two and two together. Dad had thought he was doing the right thing in introducing his friend to the magical world, to sharing the library with him—but the magical world had cast him out, leaving him bitter and alone. Dad leaving the library behind to be with Mum had been the last straw.

Maurice held out the book of questions. I didn't move. "I won't be much help if the manticore eats me. Can you confirm he's not standing outside the door?"

He glanced over his shoulder. "I'm alone. The curse has switched back to that awful parody of Roger's life story again."

My heart twisted. My aunts were trapped under the curse, unable to help me. Fuelled by a new resolve, I took the book from him and walked out of the cage, into the labyrinth of the third floor.

"Go on," he said. "End this."

I have to stall him. He probably didn't even know how to use the book to get into the question room, but once I did so, there was nothing to stop him from following me.

"What made you pick this curse?" I asked. "It's not under your control and you're at its mercy as much as the rest of us are. But then again, you don't have any magic yourself. You weren't even mentioned in the book. I guess you weren't that important, huh."

He made a low, furious noise. "Open the blasted book."

I held the book up to eye level, and said, "Stand back. It sometimes explodes."

He took one step back, then narrowed his eyes. "You're having me on."

I'd already broken into a dead sprint, running for a shortcut I knew led down to the lobby. Curse or no curse, he didn't know the library's layout as well as I did. If I could just get to my family—

"I wouldn't," he said. "Otherwise it won't end well for her, will it?"

I stopped mid-step, and my heart dropped into my shoes. A short distance away from us stood Mum, looking as solid as the two of us.

"Do you think I can't harm her?" he said. "You're wrong. The curse is now in full effect, and it's becoming real. *She's* becoming real, Rory."

At her side stood Dad. No—not Dad, not the person I'd known. Yet he looked exactly like him, as though the spell had plucked the image of my father fresh from my own memories. Or rather, *his* memories. This Dad looked younger. Younger than me, even. The same age he'd been when he'd brought Maurice into the library, excited to introduce him to the magical world.

"He could have saved your mother, you know," Maurice said. "But he chose not to. The same way he could have made the magical world accept me, yet he chose to let your fellow witches and wizards cast me out instead."

My throat closed up as Mum turned in my direction. I hadn't seen her looking so alive since before the cancer that eventually took her life. Perhaps magic could have spared her from death, but Dad hadn't had that choice. Maurice was wrong.

Dad stepped to Mum's side. "Come here, Rory," he said.

"You—" I choked off. "You died. Both of you died."

"Not in this world," said Mum. "Here, I came back to the magical world, and I lived. Because of you."

I squeezed my eyes shut. "Dad never brought his wand with him. There was no way to save you. No way to save himself."

"And do you agree with those rules, Rory?" asked Maurice.

I opened my eyes. "Dad would have broken the rules if magic could have saved Mum's life. He was willing to break the law to help a friend. Of course he would have done so again if there was any chance it would stop cancer from killing Mum." I didn't doubt that an inch. "He didn't help you because you cast *yourself* out and turned bitter and hateful. You did this to yourself."

Maurice's eyes narrowed. "You won't escape this, Rory. The curse has already taken your cousins, and it will soon spread outside the library. Imagine what will happen when the rest of the town finds out your father was the one responsible for the curse. They may already have guessed. I can still put a stop to it, you know. Just give me your father's wand and all will be forgiven."

So that's what he wants. To cast himself as the hero. But it wouldn't work, because I didn't *know* where my dad's wand was hidden, if it even still existed at all.

"I don't know where it is," I told him.

"But the book of questions does, doesn't it?" he said. "I'm told there isn't a single question it can't answer."

"That's not true," I said. "It's failed to answer my questions before. My dad probably told you otherwise because he didn't know. Even my aunts don't know everything about it."

"Then you'll never escape, Aurora," he said.

Think, Rory. Letting him into that room was out of the question—not while the curse was still in effect. But Dad *had* left his wand here in the library. And while things might often disappear in the library, nothing was lost forever.

I raised the book of questions. Maurice leaned forwards eagerly, and I hit him over the head with the book as hard as I could.

Then I ran. His furious shouts pursued me as I pelted towards the illusion of my dad—now interacting with the copies of my aunts. He turned around as I skidded to a halt next to him.

"What's the rush, Rory?" he asked.

He can see me. He's real enough to know who I am.

Maurice's shouts echoed behind me. I gave Dad a pleading look. "He wants your wand, Dad. Don't give it to him."

His eyes widened. "My wand. I left it in the library..."

"Yes?" I said quickly. "Where did you leave it?"

"I have it right here." He pulled it out of his pocket.

Of course. If this version of my dad was becoming real, then so was his wand. Or a version of it, anyway. Whatever the case, it might be enough.

"Please give it to me," I said. "It's the only way to stop him."

He hesitated, then he pressed the stick of wood into my hand. "I trust you, Rory."

I gripped the wand, which felt as real as any I'd handled in the wand shop. More, if anything, but that might be the terror pounding in my chest as Maurice strode closer.

I held the wand out, and a rush of energy flowed through my veins, tingling up my right arm to my shoulder. Sparks flew from the end. *Whoa.*

Maurice's mouth tightened. "Good. Now give it to me."

"I won't." Real or not, the wand sure *felt* solid, and the

sparks were proof enough that it would work for me. I raised the wand, waved it in the same way I'd been practising for weeks, and the thief flew back into the bookshelves with a deafening crash.

"Sorry, but the wand chose me." Sparks flew from the end, as if to accentuate my words.

Maurice let out a hoarse scream and hurtled towards me—but suddenly my dad was there, blocking the way. "Do you really want to do this, Maurice?"

"Roger." Maurice's eyes widened. "You're… real?"

"Real enough." Dad picked up the book of questions and tossed it to me. "Now it's up to you, Rory."

Right. I waved the wand, conjuring a rope to tie Maurice's feet together the same way I'd seen Aunt Adelaide do when she needed to bind up a particularly adventurous paperback.

Then I took the book of questions in hand. "I wish to enter the forbidden room."

At once, I tumbled headfirst into nothingness, the wind roaring in my ears. Then I landed in the square room with the blank walls.

Sylvester sat in the centre of the room, looking bedraggled. "About time someone came to rescue me!" he grumbled. "I've been waiting on tenterhooks for that evil little man to come in here."

"Don't worry, he won't," I said. "I need to know what he did with my cousins. And my aunts."

"Your cousins? They'll show up when the curse is undone," he said. "As for your aunts… I *suppose* I can lend a hand, if you get me out of here."

Darkness fell, and so did I. The next thing I knew, I lay flat on my back in the lobby. Beside me, the scene with my two aunts and my grandmother played out. My dad was presumably further back, watching Maurice. *This is seriously confusing.*

I climbed to my feet and walked towards my two aunts. They paused, and even Grandma turned to look at me. "And who might you be?"

"I'm Rory." I turned to Aunt Candace. "You set a spell loose in the library. I need you to undo it."

She blinked at me. "You look just like me, but I don't have children. Neither did Roger, last time I checked."

Oh, no. It was the version of them from the alternate world. They thought they were twenty-something years younger and that my dad was still alive. As for me, I didn't exist in this version of the world. I hadn't been born yet.

"I'm, er, your distant cousin," I said. "The lost cousin. Candace, one of your spells has escaped again."

"Has it?" she said.

"Yes, up on the third floor." Crossing my fingers behind my back, I made my way through the stacks. After a moment, she followed.

I stopped walking. Mum blocked my path to the stairs.

"Mum... what are you doing?" I asked.

"Helping you." She held out the copy of *The Adventures of Werewolves in Cyberland.* Aunt Candace looked at the cover, bemused.

"That looks *interesting,*" she commented. "Hmm. Not a bad idea for a title."

"Aunt—I mean, Candace!" I said. "Please, can you undo the curse on the book. You're the one who cast it, and it attached itself to that title."

"Oh yes, the Manifestation Curse." She took the book,

muttering to herself. "Tricky… I might need Roger's help for this one. Roger!"

"Yes?" Dad approached us, and my heart jumped into my throat again. I was with both my parents for what was likely the last time in my life. When the curse was undone, they'd disappear.

His hands were on the book, and he started to mutter under his breath, too. Around us, the library spun, its shelves blurring together…

"Dad."

He turned to me. "Do I know you?"

Argh. The curse is taking hold again. The spell kept back-tracking, kept replaying events, and it would do until there were dozens of versions of my parents running around. But only one of me.

Only I could end this.

"You will," I said. "I'm your daughter. You and Mum's. I know you're under Aunt Candace's spell and you're not real, but…"

"Of course you're our daughter." He stepped to Mum's side, his hands outstretched. I took their hands, and they held onto mine—

And then they were gone.

16

I stood for a moment, hands outstretched, tears stinging my eyes. One fell, then another.

"There it is!" Aunt Candace said, in triumphant tones. "Tricky curse, that... why are you crying?"

I wiped my eyes with the back of my hand. "Do you not remember? Just then, you were convinced you were twenty-five years younger."

"I *wish* I was twenty-five years younger," she said. "Right, Adelaide?"

Aunt Adelaide looked at me, then at the book of questions. "What is going on here?"

"For a start, you two were stuck under the curse's spell, Cass and Estelle are missing, and the person responsible is tied up somewhere over there." I pointed across the ground floor. "Maurice. He did it, but my dad—he helped me."

"Maurice?" said Aunt Candace. "Rory—why are you holding Roger's wand?"

I looked down at the wand in my hand. "Because he

gave it to me. It'll probably disappear along with the rest of the curse..."

Aunt Adelaide stared at my hand. "The curse *has* stopped. The wand's real."

"But... that can't be right."

"The wand was in the curse." Aunt Candace hooted with laughter. "That sounds like Roger, all right."

I sank to the floor, exhausted and emotionally drained. "I don't know where Cass and Estelle ended up."

A shout drew my attention over the bookshelves. Aunt Adelaide waved her wand and levitated Maurice into view. "So it is you," she said. "You foolish boy. What have you done to yourself?"

He glared at her. "You deserve to be punished, not me. I only wanted to take what I rightfully deserved."

"We did you a kindness in sending you away," she said, a touch of sadness in her voice. "I'm sorry to say you won't find the inside of a cell as appealing as the rest of the magical world, but it's no more than you deserve."

The next few hours were a flurry of activity as we returned the library to a state fit for visitors. Edwin showed up not long later, took one look at the thief and ordered his troll guards to take him away.

"Aren't you going to tell him Aunt Candace created the curse?" said Cass, who'd shown up on the third floor along with Estelle, and had had to charge around catching the manticore and returning it to its cage.

"I think we'll spare him," said Aunt Adelaide. "It is Christmas, after all."

"And the curse helped out in the end." I gave the wand a flick to return more books to the shelves, thrilling at the ease at which it obeyed my commands, as simple as tapping a word in my Biblio-Witch Inventory.

"Yes, and you have a wand now," said Aunt Candace. "I knew you had it in you."

"Speaking of my dad," I said. "Why didn't anyone tell me about Maurice? You never told me my dad invited his best friend here and then tried to get him inducted into the magical world."

Aunt Adelaide grimaced. "He was seventeen at the time, young and foolish. So were the rest of us… it seemed harmless at the time. I'm sorry for everyone he hurt."

"He got it all twisted in his head and convinced himself we deserved to be punished," I said quietly. "I feel sorry for him."

"You would," said Cass. "What did he do with Sylvester, anyway?"

"Scared him off," I said evasively. "I found him hiding."

The owl still hadn't returned from the forbidden room, but given the state of the place, nobody would notice his absence. Jet had been hiding up on the third floor, too, distracting the manticore to stop him from wrecking the bookshelves.

Step by step, the library returned to normal. I was levitating a stack of books into the reference section when the curse-breaker walked in.

"Ah," he said. "I'm sorry for disturbing you. I just wanted to tell you I didn't give anything away to Ursula Hancock. About the library."

I raised an eyebrow. "Isn't she going to jail anyway?"

"With any luck," said Mr Bennet. "Your grandmother and I might not have been fond of one another, but this town is our home, and I have no intention of people like her writing lies about any of us."

"Oh," I said, surprised. "Thanks."

Wonders would never cease. I returned to work, a spring in my step. The best part? My dad's wand worked perfectly. All the time I'd spent practising had finally paid off. Maybe Dad had been intending for me to find it all along, but I doubted it. Maurice might have wanted to claim it for himself, but in the end, he was the one who'd brought me to the wand I needed.

A stream of other visitors—and Jet's gossiping—told us that the effects of the curse were gone, the rest of the town was none the wiser, and Ursula had been unceremoniously fired from her reporting job as well as facing a hefty fine.

"We should throw a party," said Estelle. "A real one this time, without spiked champagne."

"You know… that's not a bad idea," I said. "Might want to give everyone the chance to recover from the holidays first, though."

Everything would go back to normal. Or as normal as it got in a town like Ivory Beach, anyway. Humming under my breath, I returned to the front desk… and spotted a note lying there.

It was written in unfamiliar, looping handwriting: *We have left town. Do not contact my apprentice again.*

The Grim Reaper.

ABOUT THE AUTHOR

Elle Adams lives in the middle of England, where she spends most of her time reading an ever-growing mountain of books, planning her next adventure, or writing. Elle's books are humorous mysteries with a paranormal twist, packed with magical mayhem.

She also writes urban and contemporary fantasy novels as Emma L. Adams.

Find Elle on Facebook at https://www.facebook.com/pg/ElleAdamsAuthor/

Made in the USA
Monee, IL
20 June 2023